LIARS

It never pays
to tell a lie —
ever!

LIARS

by

Nancy

Nancy Craddock

For Josh Craddock, my son,
a man who is truthful,
compassionate and kind.
Always.

© 2016
Nancy Cadle Craddock
www.nancycadlecraddock.com

SelfPubBookCovers.com/RLSather
First Edition: April 2016

One lie begets another.

Anonymous

CHAPTER 1

THE FIRST LIE AND THEN SOME

Please don't die, Mama. Not today. Tomorrow maybe, but not today.

"Guess I'll be leaving now. The bell's gonna ring in twenty minutes or so and Miss Caldwell likes us sixth graders to be on time. Says we're the oldest and ought to set an example for the younger ones."

"What day is it?"

"Tuesday. Nurse Day. I'll leave the door unlocked. You holler real loud for her to come on in, okay? Now don't forget." *Nurse… ha! Some nurse.* She hadn't done a thing yet, except talk about snatching me off to *The Home for the Needy*. She didn't even have the decency to let me hope that Mama would get back to the same as she was before the birth of the baby.

"You rest, Mama I'll bring you something to eat later."

"Bayou, wait! I hear the baby crying. Fetch her to me, son."

Here we go again. "No, Mama. She's not. I just gave her a bottle. She's sleeping now but I'll look in on her on my way out just the same." *No baby, unless you count a dead*

1

one laying 'neath the ground. Try not to cry. Time for school. Anyway, tears ain't gonna bring Mama's baby back, that's for sure.

"You're a good son, Bayou. You make me real proud."

"Thanks. May stop at Billy Baxter's on my way home."

"That name don't ring a bell."

"Remember? I told you. They're the new folks over on Maple. Mrs. Baxter said she hopes the two of you can get together as soon as you're up and about."

Mama smiled. It was small one, but it was there. Mama didn't smile often so just seeing it made me feel better about going off to school.

"Yep, Mama, Mrs. Baxter has sure taken a shine to me. In fact, she's always making me stay and eat. Best food I've ever tasted. She said she wished she had another son like me. I guess she'd have me living there if she could. Billy and I are practically like brothers, him being an only child and all." *Liar.*

No Billy.

No Baxters.

No food.

I searched Mama's face, wanting to believe she didn't look as tense as she did earlier, but her breathing was still labored. Her feeble-looking smile was soon replaced with her ever-more-frequent frown.

I should have stopped halfway through my little speech instead of laying it on so thick. Does she know I lie? Maybe, maybe not.

"Be good to people, son, no matter what."

"I will, Mama."

2

"Love you, Bayou."

"Love you, Mama." *Quick kiss... out the door... hard to leave.*

My usual walk to school never took more than ten minutes. Today, it took twenty. I kept dragging my feet. Should I go back? What for? Nothin, I could do, not really.

The night the baby was born, Carl Broom's mom said, "Some women are plum worn out 'fore they even give birth. Your mama was one of 'em. Is there someone you can go live with if'n she don't improve?"

"Yes," I lied. "My daddy's people out back of Monroe. They've been hankering to have me around for some time."

"What's their name?"

"Same as me - Brown. They're a fer piece out of town and do all their shopping the other way, over in Madison, not Monroe like the people here in Gratis do." *More lies.*

"I reckon that explains it then. Are you alright? Would you like for someone to stay here with you tonight? I could send Carl over."

"No, ma'am. I'm fine. Besides, Mama is here. Thanks for coming. I didn't know who else to turn to... that is until my relatives can get here." *Don't fidget. Try to look calm, sure of things.*

"Alrighty then. Fetch me if you need anything." With that, she gathered up various instruments and was out the door.

That was the day I started lying. Seems like I was real good at it from the start. Didn't seem wrong since my back was against the wall. Of course, a lie is a lie. No

3

excuse. I'd have to answer for them all one day, according to Preacher Wilcox. I swear some Sundays, it seemed like he was talking just to me.

Guess I'd worry about all of that later. Right now I had to worry about taking care of Mama and staying clear of *The Home for the Needy*.

To make matters worse, I didn't dare miss school. They came lookin' for you if you were gone too long.

People don't take too kindly to kids being raised without running water, food or heat. I'm not saying that they pitch in to make it not so, only that they don't want to know that it's happening just down the street. I guess that's why they built *The Home* - for ones like me.

No, I couldn't afford to have no one come looking for me, that's for sure.

CHAPTER TWO

END OF THE LINE

The hands on Mrs. Caldwell's clock crept from one hour to the next. Slow torture. I considered bolting out the door and running for home. Should have stayed home. Would have too, if it hadn't been "Nurse Day". Wouldn't do for the nurse to think things were so bad, I could go to school or stay home if I wanted - just the same.

When I wasn't thinking about running out of the classroom, I daydreamed about walking up our drive and waving a cheery hello to Mama, healthy... happy. I imagined her in a flower garden near the mailbox. Now, wouldn't that be something? Not only Mama outside… but a flower garden, to boot.

I would be wearing clothes that weren't faded or too small. My shirt would have every button and my pants would have a zipper that didn't get stuck on the way up.

Mama and I would enter our freshly painted house and talk about how silly our worries and fears had been. Then we would eat cake with icing and make plans for the weekend.

It was a great daydream - while it lasted. But it

didn't last long. Every time Mama got up from the table to put the cake away, she turned her back on me. Without warning, I could almost feel my heart skip a beat. Worse, that's when thoughts about burying Mama crept in and swept the dream away.

Death… digging. Not complaining, but it took me nearly half a day to dig a grave for a tiny baby. Georgia red clay ain't easy digging. Then again, I didn't have anything but a big soup spoon to work with. No shovel. I wasn't sure I could dig a regular-sized grave without nothing but a spoon. *Worry about that when the time comes.*

Okay… so… I'm not that big for an eleven-year-old but I have a lot of strength in my arms from working summers hauling boxes of apples from the orchard out on the Reinquist farm all the way through a shallow creek to the barn. Once there, I'd wait while the truck wobbled back from town for the next load. Then, I lifted crates of apples in the bed of the truck as the truck's motor whined and sputtered as it waited to go back into town. As the truck bounced down the road, I'd be making my way back to the orchard for more crates of apples. When the water in the creek bed was especially low, I'd use a wheelbarrow and bring back as many crates as it would hold. If there were several of us working that day, we'd often have to wait for the truck to come back in sight. Funny, the hard part was the waiting; not the picking, hauling or loading. It was pretty much that way now - the waiting.

Even if I had the strength to bury Mama, it was the actual doing of it that worried me.

I prayed if Mama died today, it was before the nurse made her rounds. Then, they might send someone to help with burying her and do whatever else they did. Hopefully, then they'd be on their way and that'd be the last I'd see *the* nurse.

Otherwise… if word got out I was all alone, who knows what hour of the day, one of the nurses, or anyone, would come back for me. My greatest fear was that I could be snatched right out of my house any day of the week and sent to *The Home* without warning.

It was hard to stand the worry of that happening from one day to the next. As it was, I nearly jumped out-of-my-skin now whenever anyone behind me coughed or so much as closed a book in school.

My prayer was that I'd have a warning and could talk myself out of going anywhere… with anyone.

Movement out of the corner of my eye brought me back to the classroom. Carl passed a note to me asking if I was okay. I nodded and gave a thumbs-up.

Carl returned it with a smile from the corner of his bruised lip as he and the rest of my classmates stood up and shuffled toward our classroom door.

Carl walked toward me, saying, "Man, I'm hungry. I didn't think lunchtime would ever get here."

"Lunch? Didn't we eat already?"

Carl stepped ahead of me, saying "You're a funny guy, Bayou. Real funny."

I took my place behind Norma Adams and shook my head "no" when Carl motioned for me to jump in line ahead of him.

"Another time," I muttered.

"Sure. Walk home like usual?"

"You bet," I mouthed back to him along with the best goofy face I could make. We both broke out

7

laughing.

Darn rule. Oh, well. I wouldn't leave Norma anyway. Then she'd be the only free lunch in our class. Not that I like her or anything, just wouldn't feel right abandoning her to the pity looks and "sorry-for-you" stares from everyone else in the cafeteria.

Never one to miss a chance to complain, Norma turned around. "I don't know why you act so silly. I'm sick and tired of being last in line. Don't you think it's rather strange that they run out of the good food every day just before the two of us get up to the counter?"

"I doubt they do it on purpose. It's just that we're the last ones in the entire school to eat. It'll probably be different next year at the Junior High. Makes me kinda sad, not much longer to endure our usual, peanut-butter sandwiches," I said half-laughing, hoping to calm her down. I didn't want any more attention drawn to the fact that the two of us were the only "free lunch" kids in the entire sixth grade.

"Well, we may have to eat peanut-butter sandwiches every day but I still don't see why we have to be last."

"Mrs. Caldwell said that the cafeteria cashier wants us lined up that way. Makes it easier to keep the records straight if we're last. So, here we are: Adams… and Brown… ta da."

"Maybe. I don't know. I'd just like to get a taste of something other than peanut-butter once in a while… here and at home."

I felt the same way, but for some reason the words wouldn't come out. A lump had started to form in the back of my throat. I wanted to scream, "At least you

8

don't have to worry that someone is going to see you wrap up half of your sandwich every day in a worn-out piece of aluminum foil."

Shouldn't complain. Mr. Jordan, the custodian was always saving things from lunchroom trays for me. No, it wasn't unusual for me to take home a banana, an orange or an apple. Some days, he let me know with a wink that he'd left something special in the boiler room for me.

After school, I would stall around until everyone was gone and then dart inside the stuffy room. On top of a large wooden crate, I'd find something like a jar of jelly or a loaf of bread. Every once in a while, I'd find a couple of pieces of cake or slices of pie!

I couldn't bring myself to think about living on nothing but hand-outs very long. It made me sad for me. Mama, too. It seemed likely that Mrs. Caldwell was in on leaving things there, too. I wanted to tell her how much it meant to me, but every time I tried, tears would puddle in my eyes. Rather than look like a big-bawling baby, I kept quiet. Even so, I think she knew how much I appreciated it... for both me... and Mama. At least, I hope she knew. After all, she was a teacher - wise.

CHAPTER THREE

THE LONG SLEEP

Finally, the bell. Even though my eyes had hardly left the big round clock on my classroom wall all day, I dreaded going home. I knew Mama was gone. I don't know how I knew, but I did. The air felt different somehow. I felt different – scared and unsure.

After a couple of playful jabs with classmates at the water fountain and the usual tugging and shoving of books in and out of our lockers, several of us walked to the end of Maple. Kids peeled off along the way until only Carl walked with a slight limp beside me. The two of us trudged uphill past the laundry mat and in no time at all, we reached the end of his driveway where we went through our normal parting slapstick comedy.

"See y'a Carl," I'd say with a light jab to his shoulder.

"Not if I see you first," he'd answer with a little harder jab back to my shoulder.

We'd do this back and forth a whole lot of times. Each jab a tad bit harder than the one before. It always ended when his step-daddy came out on the porch and yelled for Carl to get inside and for me to go on home. Then, I would trudge on alone.

I always dreaded going past the Blue Parrot Inn. There were always broken bottles and bits of glass mixed among worn and chipped concrete once passed as a sidewalk - about a hundred years ago, probably. To make matters worse, there was always some seedy person hanging around. As always, I walked with my head down and tried not to look around too much.

Eventually, our dusty mailbox would come into view. It was old and battered, pretty much like everything else we owned. Every time the wind blew, I expected to see it fly past or plop to the ground. No matter. We didn't get mail. We didn't send any either.

One thing for sure, Mama was pretty proud of the fact that we weren't renters. Whenever the subject came up, I merely nodded in agreement. Truthfully, I figured the only reason we owned the place was no one else in their right mind would want to live in such a tiny, worn-out shack.

Mama insisted that her daddy could have sold it and made money on the deal but I wasn't so sure of that. I think he gave it to us just to be done with the place. Sure seemed like he was done with us, too. He never came around, hadn't for years. When pressed, Mama admitted if she had to guess, he'd moved off somewhere.

I kicked a stone and started up the driveway which was mostly weedy clumps of red clay in some places and fine red powder in others. Nothing lasts, at least not on my run-down side of town.

The nurse was standing in the yard - smoking. I was right. She never came this late in the day and she definitely wouldn't have stayed this long. I turned at the sound of a car engine. *A shiny black hearse.*

I darted behind a shrub and watched as it pulled slowly up our driveway and came to a stop. As it passed, I could see my reflection in the car's shiny black paint. I looked like an
animal caught in a trap.

The nurse didn't waste any time bossing the driver around. He, in turn, told another man "to get a move on".

"Basic routine, nothing more," the nurse snapped. "Not a paying customer. Expense will be covered by the state and we have our limits, you know."

"No problem lady," the driver replied gruffly.

"Not my rules, state guidelines. Goodness, that kid should be here by now. I need to see if he's got some place to go before I can leave here."

Step up. Tell her you're all set. Get her out of here. With trembling legs, I slid out from behind the shrub and walked up the driveway as if I had just arrived.

"Oh, there you are. Come on up here, boy."

"Yes, ma'am." *No matter what, don't let her see you cry.*

"Reckon you can see that your mama has been called on high," the nurse said without any emotion.

"Yes, ma'am. I see that." *Hold back the tears.*

The nurse took one long puff before flicking her cigarette butt to the ground. "Exactly where is the rest of your family? Supposing you got some, that is."

"My dad and his new family live outside of Monroe. In fact, my dad's picking me up today for ball practice. Should be here any minute now." *Look down the driveway as if a car is going to come speeding up any minute.*

About that time, the men came out carrying a stretcher. From under the white sheet, Mama's weathered hand dangled down. I clasped it in mine and walked alongside until I had to let go and the hearse door went shut.

One of the men put his hand on my shoulder and said, "I'm real sorry about your mother, son. Are you sure you've got someone coming for you?

I nodded. *Don't break down, not yet. Later.* The other man patted my head and then they were gone. *Let's go inside our freshly painted house and laugh about how worried we were over nothing and what a big mistake it all was.*

"Well, at least Mama's leaving here, riding in the back of a big shiny car. That's something, don't you think." *Drats. Had I actually said that aloud? Not myself today. Doubted I would ever be again.*

"Umm… yes, I guess. Sure, that's something," the nurse muttered in reply. Then she made a point of looking at her watch and back down the driveway. "Are you sure that daddy of yours is on his way?"

"Oh, yes ma'am. He should be here any minute now."

"I gotta get supper ready for my own kid and husband. Got a daughter 'bout your age. Can't stay here long."

Get her and her old smelly cigarettes out of here. Lie. Any lie will do, but make it a good one - in honor of Mama. "Well, sometimes, he stops on the way to bring me French fries and a milkshake. I'll be fine. Honest, he'll be here any minute now."

"I got to write this up… on top of coming way out here. All this takes time, you know."

"I understand. Thanks for everything." *Everything, ha! NOTHING is more like it. Should tell her so. But can't.*

14

"Well, 'speck I'll go ahead and leave. Need to get home."

"Son, be good to people - no matter what." I didn't want to be good to anybody, especially the nurse but Mama's words forced me to offer the nurse my hand. "Thank you."

"My job, you know," the nurse said as she moved something gold and shiny from her hand to her coat pocket before reaching out her had to shake mine. *Funny time to be hiding something. What? No matter. Mama's gone.*

The nurse quickly let go of my hand and seemed even more anxious to get away than before. *Hiding something. Familiar. But what? Should know, but don't. Think on it later.*

Finally, she left in a cloud of red dust. I kicked the screen door but it was warped so badly, it barely opened. Chips of old paint fluttered to the ground as the bottom of the door scraped against the crooked porch floor. I gave it another kick - much harder this time and stepped into stillness and shadows. It was over. Now what?

Why today? Tomorrow would have been better, a whole lot better or maybe the day after that day. Why today of all days? A regular old Tuesday.

Ah, bet you waited for Nurse Day. Were you worried I couldn't do the job? Not sure myself. Yes, riding off in a shiny black car was far better. Won't forget you, Mama. Never-ever.

CHAPTER FOUR

MISSING MAMA

I waited all day to get back home so that I could cry. But now that I was home, I couldn't. Imagine that. No tears. Only silence. Late October, cold already. I thought about going outside to scrounge up some firewood. Too tired. No matches anyway.

Instead, I crawled into Mama's bed. Whether or not, it was really still warm didn't matter. It felt warm to me. I pulled mama's quilt over my face and that's when I began to cry.

I must have fallen asleep because the next thing I knew was the sound of a dog's bark off in the darkness. Had to go - bad, even if it was still scary dark outside. I lay there, hoping the feeling would go away but it didn't. So, I wrapped the quilt around my shoulder and sprinted out the door to make a quick trip to "Little Egypt". Then, I dashed back inside and jumped back into Mama's bed.

Fully awake now, I lay in the darkness, thinking. I needed a plan and one that didn't involve *The Home*. No, sir - not one little bit. Carl said it wasn't that bad of a place. According to his cousin Earl, they fed you. Three squares a day - or so he said. Sounded a bit far-fetched to me. One maybe, but not three. Then again, Earl spent half a year there before his daddy came back and moved them all out of town. So, maybe he had it right. No matter. *The Home* wern't for me.

Bad enough to be poor, downright embarrassing to live on charity and have everyone know that you do. Might as well, sit on the street corner and hold a cap in your hand. No, I'd make my own way. I didn't know exactly how at the moment. I'd have to think on it hard - real hard.

Somewhere among all of those thoughts, I guess I fell back to sleep because I dreamed about tossing pennies in the fountain over in Monroe. I dreamed the pennies were hitting the water with a quick thud, thud, thud instead of splash, splash, splash.

From a drowsy distance, I realized the thuds were coming from the front door. Still groggy, I thought for a split second, my French fries and milkshake had arrived. Seeing as how I never knew my daddy, I doubted it was the fries but I darted to the door just the same.

I opened it quickly, only to find my sixth grade teacher starring back at me.

"Are you alright?" Mrs. Caldwell asked.

"Yes, ma'am."

"Bayou, I am really sorry about your mother," Mrs. Caldwell said with a quick hug. "They said she died peacefully in her sleep. A blessing, for sure."

Really? No one told me. At least that's a comfort to know.

"Yes, ma'am."

"Bayou, even though your grief is still fresh, I hope you'll come on back and join us tomorrow. If you do, don't worry about studying your words for the

18

spelling test."

"Yes, ma'am." *Spelling test? Spelling tests were always on Friday. What happened to Wednesday and Thursday? Musta slept through 'em. Just as well.*

"Is there some place I can put this down?" Mrs. Caldwell asked softly.

Suddenly, I realized she was holding a box that smelled like fried chicken. *Better than make-believe fries, that's for sure.*

"Smells mighty good, Mrs. Caldwell. Thank you." I sure hoped she wouldn't barge right in. *House too small, too shabby.*

"Then, we'll see you tomorrow?"

"Yes, ma'am. I'll be there."

After she left, I realized she didn't ask where I was going to live or how I was going to survive. Just as well. I had a plan but it would take a lot of luck and I might not be able to pull it off.

Livin' in an orphanage wasn't for me; no way, no how. I was going to raise myself. And anyway, there wasn't any other choice. There never had been a daddy with fries and a milkshake.

Not likely to be one now.

CHAPTER FIVE

OUT OF THE BLUE

It's funny how life wraps itself around you and carries you along. Everything was pretty much back to the same as before. Outwardly, that is. If you didn't look too close. Inside, it felt like my heart had a big empty hole in the middle of it, like a jigsaw puzzle - the kind you find in someone's trash or at a yard sale. You know without even trying, you can never put it together because too many of the pieces are missing.

After Mama passed, there wasn't any need to hurry home after school each day, so I stayed and helped Mr. Jordan, the school janitor. In fact, Mr. Jordan and me had us a regular routine. We never officially divided the chores or really talked about it much. It just kinda happened. I gathered up trash from one side of the building and he the other. After we got all the trash hauled out back, I mopped one side of the cafeteria while he did the other. Next, I checked the stalls in the boys' room and put toilet paper on the empty rolls while he did the same in the girls' room.

Our grand finale was mopping our way down the main hallway until we ended up back at the boiler room where the whole thing had started in the first place.

After squeezing out our mops and leaning them against the cement wall to dry, we went out the door, I walked around the right side of the building, making sure every window was locked while he checked the ones on the left.

No matter how cold it was or how hard the wind blew, we'd sit for a minute or two on the front steps. Sometimes, we didn't say nothin'. Other times, we did. Even then, when we talked, we didn't decide the fate of the world or anything much. Mainly, we chatted-on about the weather or something like whether or not it was better to be left-handed or right. Often, Mr. Jordan would ask me if Carl's dad was still drinking and how things were going for Carl. I always nodded and said "bout the same".

Fridays were different. Instead of parting ways on the steps of the school, I'd walk all the way home with Mr. Jordan 'cause I had a standin' invitation for dinner every Friday night. Mrs. Jordan told me so herself.

So, instead of being the beginning of a long and hungry weekend, Friday night turned out to be the happiest time of the week. I wanted to tell the Jordans so, but something else always came out like, "These sure are good pinto beans, Mrs. Jordan."

"Why, thank you, Bayou. The only problem is I always cook too much."

"From the look of what's left in the pot, I can see that, ma'am."

"I'm hoping you'll take some home with you. Sure would help a lot."

"I could do that. In fact, I can take just about all you got. Providing that is, you're not plannin' on having

22

them again tomorrow night."

"I declare, I don't believe that I care to eat pintos again for a week."

"Well, I don't mind eating the same thing twice and then some," I replied.

Mr. Jordan added, "Well then that's settled. I'm putting the leftover pintos in jars and they're going home with you, Bayou."

It was a good thing, too. It was a long time from a peanut-butter sandwich at noon on Friday until the next one at lunch the following Monday at school.

I wanted to repay Mrs. Jordan but she said helping Mr. Jordan, or Ed as she called him, get things squared away at school was payment enough. Truth be known, I'd help anyway.

Even though I didn't have running water at home, I was determined to take the pinto jars back to Mrs. Jordan clean. Finally, I figured how to do it.

I'd take one to school each day and stuff it in my desk until Wednesday. That was the day Mr. Jordan left school early in the afternoon and came back later to finish up. The time in-between, he drove Preacher Wilcox over to Monroe for a weekly meeting with some church folks and a couple of preachers there. Mr. Jordan spent the time picking up cleaning supplies for the Baptist church here.

In the beginning, it was supposed to be a paying job but Mr. Jordan said it seemed downright sinful to charge one preacher to pray with another preacher for the lost and afflicted. So, he did it for free.

As it turned out then, Wednesdays were my opportunity to wash the jars in complete privacy. I'm ashamed to say it, but sometimes I even washed my clothes in the bathroom sink, too. Someone must have noticed. Things like toothpaste, soap and deodorant were left in the boy's bathroom for me most every Wednesday after the rest of the students left for the day.

Afterwards, I would take my clothes to the boiler room and toss them over a long rope that stretched from one end of the room to the other. It was always hot and stuffy in there. By the time Mr. Jordan got back and we got the trash emptied and floors mopped, my clothes were dry. In fact, somewhere in there, Mr. Jordan and I started playing basketball with my stuff. A grocery sack became a hoop and my folded clothes became a ball. When the game was done, everything was back in my bag, ready to go.

The only dark spot was when Mr. Jordan and his wife had to leave town for the weekend to check on his sister and her kids down by Macon. Those were some mighty long weekends, I can tell you. I don't want to dwell on it too much, other than to say it was a big relief to see Monday morning roll around.

One Friday, when I was down in the dumps about not seeing Mr. Jordan or much of anyone else until Monday, Mrs. Caldwell asked me to stay after school.

"Bayou, I've been wondering if you might have some time this weekend to do a friend a favor?"

"Sure. What do you want me to do, Mrs. Caldwell?"

"Nelda Reader at the library asked me to recommend someone to help with Story Hour on Saturday mornings. I thought about you."

"What would I have to do?"

"She needs someone to read to the younger children and help them find a book or two. Interested?"

"I reckon I am."

"That's marvelous. Nelda will be so pleased," Mrs. Caldwell said with a smile.

I got to thinking about being in front of an audience, even if it was only a bunch of little kids and Added, "Uh, um, can I wear my everyday clothes?"

"Goodness, yes. You wouldn't want to wear anything nice there anyway, especially with little ones crawling all around," she answered with a smile.

Feeling reassured, I told her to go ahead and volunteer me. So, she wrote a note "This is the young man that I told you about. He is the best I have to send."

I don't know why and I sure didn't expect to, but I started bawling, just like a baby. Mrs. Caldwell sat down by my side and put her arm around my shoulder.

"It's okay, Bayou. Things are going to turn out just fine. You'll see."

I didn't know if I believed her or not, but it sure was good to hear. I dried my eyes and headed toward the library. On the way, I got to worrying about the crying starting up again. I wondered if I should wait a while before entering. But I couldn't wait. For some reason, I felt drawn there.

When I located Miss Reader, she was behind a stack of books. Through thick dark glasses and under fuzzy red hair, she peered over the pages of *Grasshoppers are Great* at me. I took off my cap and handed her my note as I said, "Mrs. Caldwell sent me."

"Wonderful, absolutely wonderful. Can you start

this Saturday?"

"Yes, ma'am."

"Oh good. By the way, it's a paying job you know. Not much. Two dollars each and every Saturday. And oh, don't eat breakfast before you come. Doughnuts and orange juice will be provided."

"Really?"

She burst into laughter and said, "You bet, honey. You're gonna need a lot of energy to deal with the little munchkins."

"Yes, ma'am. I 'spect I will." I simply could not believe my luck! Two whole dollars each and every Saturday. *I might survive after all.*

That night, I dreamed I was swimming in an ocean of orange juice. Just as the current started to wash me away, Miss Reader threw me a life-preserver. As I reached for it, it turned into a giant doughnut.

In the early morning light, I tried to remember Mama's words and voice. Later, I rummaged through nearly everything - bits of this and that.

Finally, I found what I had been looking for - an old picture of mama holding me. I was baby and mama looked barely old enough to have a kid herself. I always wondered who took the snapshot. When I was little, I pretended my daddy took it. Probably not. No matter. It was comforting to look at her picture and know that she had been.

CHAPTER SIX

I'LL BE HOME FOR CHRISTMAS

The day before school let out for Christmas vacation turned out better than I expected. It snowed. It hardly ever snows in little old Gratis, Georgia. During math, Mrs. Caldwell might as well have been explaining long division in a foreign language. Finally, she dusted the chalk from her hands and said, "No one seems to be thinking straight or able to concentrate."

Boy, was she right. Trips to the pencil sharpener, trash can or tissue box were really just an excuse to look out the window - yet again.

The girls whispered words like "hot chocolate" and "sleigh ride".

We boys picked our teams and planned our strategy for a long hoped for, much awaited, all-out snowball fight.

Right before the dismissal bell, Mrs. Caldwell announced, "Class, you are all invited over to my house after school today. I thought a batch of newly baked chocolate chip cookies would be a nice way to start Christmas vacation."

At the sound of the bell, we threw on our jackets and headed out. We weren't sure throwing snowballs along the way would be allowed. So, we settled for kicking as much snow as we possibly could while we walked.

At first, we when got there, we just stood around looking at the Christmas tree. Later, when the cookies were gone, Mrs. Caldwell suggested we sit in a circle and one-by-one tell one thing that we were thankful for during the past year. She said "not that it was Thanksgiving or anything - just a good time to recollect before moving forward again".

I couldn't think of anything. Nothin'. It had been the worse year of my life. I thought about bolting for the bathroom or better yet, the front door but I sat frozen while the voices of my classmates moved quickly around the circle. Suddenly, all eyes were on me.

"Music." Dead silence. *Oh, my gosh. Whatever made me blurt out something so stupid?*

"What do you mean?" questioned Marsha.

"Music, you know, music." *What a jerk! If they laugh, I deserve it. Big dummy.*

"I like music, too - all kinds," Norma chimed in with a smile.

Carl wasn't far behind, "I whistle or hum something everywhere I go."

Everyone started talking about their favorite kind of music and in no time at all, we were all up and gathered around Mrs. Caldwell's piano. Sally Roberts sat down and started playing Christmas carols. One voice after another joined in until we ended with the loudest, most off-key rendition of "We Wish You A Merry

Christmas" ever belted out in the history of the world.

When the last verse ended, Jerry jumped up and yelled, "Snowball fight. Who's in?"

"Hey, thought we were starting in the morning," Carl said, as a slow grin spread across his face.

"Well, you thought wrong," Jerry answered. "We're starting now. Consider this a warm-up for the real thing and get ready to lose!"

"No way, Jose," Carl answered as he darted for the door.

Amid the yells and cheers, there was a mad scramble for coats, gloves, scarves and hats.

In the end, we had the "bestest snowball fight ever". It was wonderful. Eventually, night fell and one-by-one everyone headed home, tired and wet.

Mrs. Caldwell asked me to stay behind so that I could carry a plate of Christmas cookies to Maude Pruitt. Maude had never learned to drive and now that her husband was gone, she was a shut-in.

As I waited for Mrs. Caldwell to reappear from the kitchen, I debated snatching left-over pieces of cookies to stuff in my pockets. But I figured it would be the same as stealing so I didn't. *What a waste. Enough broken cookies to keep me goin' for quite awhile. Wonder what everyone would say if they knew how bad things really were at my house? Wonder if anyone already knew. I hoped not.*

When Mrs. Caldwell came back, she was carrying two plates full of Christmas cookies.

"One's for Miss Maude and the other one's for you, Bayou."

"Thank you ma'am, but you didn't have to bake me nothin', Mrs. Caldwell."

"When I get going with my bakin', I seldom know when to stop. I'd much rather give you the extras than to see them go to waste," Mrs. Caldwell said with a gentle smile.

Her words made me feel better about taking somethin' without givin' anything' back. I wasn't sure it was true or not but it sure would be a sin to toss the extra cookies away when there were kids in China starvin' to death. But before I could get out a "thank you", Mrs. Caldwell was pulling out a brightly wrapped present from under her tree.

"I 'spect Miss Maude will be pretty excited to see me show up with the cookies and a big present," I said to Mrs. Caldwell as I reached for it.

"Oh no, dear. This is for you," she stated.

"Me? You... you didn't have to get me nothin'," I stuttered as she handed the large package to me. "I don't have nothin' to give you back."

"Bayou, your sweet spirit and smile has been a year-round present to me," she replied. "Besides, you have been so good to help out in the classroom and around the school - only fair."

"I like helping out. Ain't got nothin' better to do."

"Well, that may be, but it still has meant a lot to me... and others."

I looked down at the present in my hands. Feeling as though I was dreaming, I kept muttering, "Thank you, Mrs. Caldwell. Thank you, ma'am. Thank you."

"You're more than welcome. Just some things my husband thought a boy your age might like for Christmas. I was hoping he'd get home by now so that he could meet you. Guess he's running late. He probably kept the store open for last minute holiday shoppers."

"Will you thank him for me?"

"I will... and Merry Christmas, Bayou."

"Merry Christmas and thank you, Mrs. Caldwell."

Back home, I wanted to twist off the ribbon and tear away the paper. But I didn't. If I opened my gift now, I'd have nothin' to open on Christmas morning. So I just held the box for awhile before putting it in the back corner of my closet for safe-keeping.

The thought of a wrapped Christmas present cheered me throughout the following week. It seemed like the day would never come and the week lasted forever even though I kept busy.

The first day of Christmas vacation, I spent the day doing math - sorta. Not getting a free lunch at school would mean going a little hungrier than usual. I would have to limit the amount of food I ate every day if I was going to be able to make it through the holidays. I was determined to 'mathematically make it work', as Mrs. Caldwell would say.

I scraped peanut-butter out of the jar and made fourteen scoops on a sheet of wax paper. Next, I counted the slices of bread in a bag to make sure I had enough. Then, I matched the amount of peanut-butter to the bread. The last thing I had to do was decided whether to divide the fourteen scoops. I finally decided to half them again. This way, I could eat half a sandwich for breakfast and treat myself to another one for dinner. Both sandwiches would be small but maybe my stomach wouldn't hurt too much to sleep at night.

The days were long and boring but finally Christmas morning arrived.

I decided to get cleaned up before sitting down to eat a left-over stale doughnut from Story Hour.

I wanted to make the excitement of the day last, so I fished around in Mama's night stand until I found her Bible. It fell open to the second chapter of Luke, the same verse Mama and I always read about the birth of baby Jesus every Christmas Eve.

At that moment, I knew for sure that Mama was lookin' after me even if she weren't on earth any more. I couldn't help thinking that at least I had a roof over my head. The precious baby Jesus had a bed of straw in a cold barn. Yes, things could be worse, a whole lot worse.

Finally, I couldn't wait any longer. I opened my closet door and pulled out the present from Mrs. Caldwell and eagerly removed the bow and paper.

Inside were two pairs of blue jeans along with three shirts and a sweater. I didn't know what to do or think. It was too much! Should I keep it all? It might seem rude to give some of it back.

As I wondered what I should do, my eyes fell on a handwritten note at the bottom of the box. It read simply "My husband and I really want you to have these. Merry Christmas, Boyd and Margaret Caldwell".

That settled it. Everything would stay. I tried everything on and wished I had a mirror. No matter, I knew everything looked good - real good!

I decided to walk to the Caldwell's so that I could say "thank you" in person. Even though it was cold, I didn't want to cover up my clothes so I left my tattered coat behind.

When I stepped out on the porch, I knew there really must be a Santa! On the porch were several boxes -

cereal, bread, cans of soup, pickles, tuna, and other things to eat. Socks, underwear, a flashlight, comic books, and matchbox cars spilled out of another box.

As I pulled out first one thing and then another from the boxes, I began to sob.

Someone knew.

Someone cared.

After putting everything in the kitchen, I headed toward the Caldwell's. Tears flowed as I walked, but luckily, as my steps speeded up, my jerky sobs slowed down, and by the time I reached their door, I was pretty much cried out.

Mrs. Caldwell opened the door and said, "Bayou, I declare! Is that really you?"

"Yes, ma'am. It may not look like me, but it is."

"Boyd, this is the young man I've been telling you about. Come meet my favorite student, Bayou Brown," Mrs. Caldwell said to a tall, friendly-looking man standing in the hallway behind her.

"So this is Bayou, is it?"

"Yes, sir, I am. Mighty pleased to meet you, Mr. Caldwell," I said as we shook hands.

"Margaret, you didn't tell me he was your most handsome student," Mr. Caldwell teased.

"I just came by to say my thanks," I stammered.

"I'm glad that you did. Now, that you're here, what about joining us for Christmas service?" Mrs. Caldwell asked.

"Why, I 'spect I could," I answered.

So, off to church went. Preacher Wilcox seemed mighty surprised and pleased to see me. So did several of my classmates. After the service, we stood around telling anyone who would listen what we got for Christmas.

A classmate, Marsha Thomas invited me back to church later that week for Wednesday night supper. I stalled around until I found out it was free. Then, I promised I'd show-up.

I rounded out the day by stopping by the Jordans before heading over to Carl's. All in all, it turned out to be a really good Christmas, even though I didn't get to do the one thing I wanted desperately to do - find Mama's grave.

Finding Mama could mean talking to the nurse. If the nurse sensed how likely everything was to come tumbling down around me, she might start the wheels in motion to have me sent to *The Home*.

Couldn't chance that - yet.

CHAPTER SEVEN

FLASH OF GOLD

Maybe I shouldn't tell this but I never did go back to my own bed after Mama died. Instead, I crawled into her bed to sleep at night. On the nights it was so cold I could reach out and touch my own breath, I would pull Mama's old quilt all the way up over my head. It felt good to be tucked in - secure.

And I learned a few tricks along the way. When I thought I couldn't stand the cold any longer, I'd wrap the quilt around my shoulders, shove on my shoes and run as fast as I could to the coin laundry. I'd use a couple of my Story Hour quarters to run the dryer there. As soon as it got going, I'd hop on top and lay down.

I know I looked stupid and strange, but not having my teeth chatter for a whole thirty minutes was worth it. Definitely. Besides, the place was empty that time of night, except for Carl when his step-daddy got really riled up.

One night, Carl said, "Dag nab it, angry drunks don't care what kind of weather they run you off in."

"Guess not. Want to share part of my quilt? Got a couple more Story Hour quarters if'n you want to run your own dryer," I offered.

"Nah. Keep your quarters. The dryer on the end starts every now and then when you give it a swift kick on the bottom right."

"Keep forgettin' 'bout that," I answered, as my dryer clicked off and Carl and I moved toward the end Carl could run the free dryer and I could use another quarter on one. The dryers were old and loud but if we sat on dryers close together we could talk without shouting.

Carl laughed and said, "If it doesn't warm up soon, I guess I'll stop going by your house and just head on over here instead."

"Such a funny guy!" I jabbed his shoulder and he jabbed mine right back.

That's the thing about Carl. He always made me laugh. Maybe I should have been embarrassed - sitting on a dryer in the middle of the night but I wasn't. His situation wasn't much better than mine. He did have a mother. But along with that mother, he had him a step-daddy that didn't know when to stop hittin'.

Carl's arms and legs stayed black and blue. Hardly anyone knew that but me. Carl had gotten good at covering up. He wore long pants and sleeves even during the hot summer months. And the only place the two of us would even consider for swimming was in the pond back of the Reinquist farm - far from prying eyes.

I think Mrs. Caldwell suspected something because she made a point of visiting Carl's house at least once or twice a month. Guess that was her way of trying to keep Carl's step-daddy on guard. What she didn't know was that her visits made things worse. Carl didn't have the heart to tell her and made me promise not to say anything either.

Carl's step-daddy would act all sweet and nice to Mrs. Caldwell and then he'd fly into a rage as soon as she was out of sight. He'd slap everyone in sight, especially Carl and then shout that it was nobody's business how he raised his own son and *others*. Later, when I was holding ice on some part of Carl's bruised and battered body, I'd try to cheer him up by conjuring what being an *other* meant. We finally settled on green people from some faraway galaxy.

Like Mrs. Caldwell's surprise visits, every now and then, something unexpected came my way. It happened one day after school when I needed it the most.

"Bayou, I've got a wonderful surprise for you," Mrs. Caldwell said one day after everyone else had left the room.

"For me?"

"Yes. Someone, who chooses to remain nameless, would like to pay for your lunch every day. Then, you could get the regular meal - like everyone else. Isn't that lovely?"

"Well, yes, ma'am. I guess so, but I can't," I replied. *Ah… it would be heavenly to sit with Carl and have a regular tray like the everyone else.*

I would have enjoyed sitting with Carl and eating regular-like but I figured that didn't matter as much as being there for Norma - even if it wasn't near as much fun.

"Why-ever-not?" Mrs. Caldwell questioned, sounding puzzled.

"That would put Norma the only one."

"The only one to what?"

37

"The only one to eat a peanut-butter sandwich every day. She'd feel bad." *"Be good to people" There it was again, as clear as the day Mama died. Good to hear her voice even if only in my head.*

Mrs. Caldwell thought for a moment. "Are you sure? Once I tell him that you have declined his offer, you may not have another opportunity."

"Yes, ma'am."

"Bayou, you probably won't understand this now, but every once in a while when I just about give up on the human race, someone or something comes along to reaffirm the goodness of man and my heart leaps with joy. I feel that way now."

"Yes, ma'am."

Knowing someone offered gave me a lot to smile about that night even if I didn't get regular food. Hard to explain, but just knowing that someone cared made the school's runny peanut butter and dry bread sandwiches taste better from that day on.

I pretended that *someone* was my own daddy. Maybe he couldn't come for me for fear of the government or something mysterious like that. Now, wouldn't that be something? I'd like that.

Anyway, as the days warmed up and winter started to give way to spring, I got to thinkin' how hard it must be wearing long pants and sleeves all the time. I decided if stuck by old Norma, I could surely sweat along with Carl. So, I never put back on my short sleeve shirts no more. Only fair.

That night, I had a dream about covering up. I had a hat on my head and socks on my feet. I was putting on a glove when all of a sudden, my hand opened up. A flash of gold! Only it wasn't my hand. It was the hand of the nurse. I was awake in an instant and I knew what it was the nurse was hiding from me on the day my mama died.

CHAPTER EIGHT

SORTIN' IT ALL OUT

I daydreamed about marching into the nurse's office and snatching Mama's brooch off of her smelly chest, but even I wasn't that dumb. Besides, I didn't 'spect the nurse would be wearing it in public but who knows. I doubt she'd see any trouble coming from me. Even if she didn't expect to get caught, who would believe me - the poorest kid in town?

Mama didn't own but one nice thing, and that brooch was it. Granny gave it to her before the depression and things got bad. Mama said it was valuable even in the worst of times, but even so, it tweren't never to leave the family. I guess there are some things that mean a whole lot more than firewood on a cold night.

To Mama, that brooch was worth more than a stack of firewood even when the two of us were wearing all of our clothes and still freezing half-to-death.

Mama said, "Once folks know you're poor, they got you. You can't get what you should for something if you are desperate and people know it. So, the rich end up with something of value for the price of a cheap trinket."

I replied, "Seems like the poor should pay less and

the rich pay more."

Mama's only answer was "Sadly, things don't work that way."

Mama always said that the brooch would go to my wife. Since I'm no fortune teller, who or when that might be, remains a mystery to me. In fact, I can't think of one girl in the whole town who would be interested in me. Of course, Mrs. Caldwell is the only one I'd ever see fit to marry but she's too old for me, not to mention the fact, she's already married.

At any rate, the brooch was mine, no matter what, wife-to-be or not. In fact, if'n I wanted to bury it in the backyard with my baby sister, that'd be my business. The brooch was mine, not the nurse's and I aimed to have it back. I just wasn't sure how to go about it or who would help me.

More than likely, I'd end up telling Carl - him being like kin. But then again, no telling what his step-daddy might get out of him with the belt one night and then, turn around and blab it to anyone who would listen at the Blue Parrot.

For the moment, it might be better all the way around to rely on someone else.

I figured there was only one person wise enough to help me think it all through. When that Friday evening did finally did come, I asked if I could have a private conversation with Mr. Jordan as soon as our meal was over. Mrs. Jordan didn't seem to mind and said she had some mendin' to do anyway. So, Mr. Jordan and me headed out back.

"Mr. Jordan, I have a problem. I'm not sure how to go about getting' back something that's mine."

"And just what might *that* something be?"

"My mother's brooch. The visiting nurse stole it the day my mama passed," I replied as business-like as possible. *Stick to the subject, don't cry.*

"I see."

"I mean to have it back."

"At what cost?"

"Just about any, sir. I'm not aiming to end up at *The Home* but even then, if that's what it takes. I want it back."

"Some say living at that place is a pretty heavy price to pay," he answered gravely.

"Yes, sir. I imagine it is, sir."

"What have you in mind?"

"That's just it. I don't rightly know."

"Well, it seems to me there are two things to think on. First off, if you just go and take it, it could be considered stealing on your part - through the eyes of the law, that is. Secondly, if your Mama was here today, would she want you to risk entering the orphanage over it? Of course, the decision is yours."

"Yes, sir." *Drat. A tear. Thought I was cried out. No matter. Probably just nerves, still jumpy.*

"Come closer, Bayou. I want to tell you something. No matter how smart or rich you are, life isn't fair. And you, my son, have been dealt a pretty hard blow, for sure. Be that as it may, what really matters is how you deal with people. That's where real happiness lies. Even if you get the brooch back - which you might, it ain't never going bring your mama back, baby. Not in a million years."

I didn't say anything for several minutes. I knew

43

he was right. Even so, I wanted to bring her brooch back home where it belonged.

"I know, but I want it back," I said with more force than I intended. I never knew how my voice was going to come out anymore. Maybe I squeaked at times because my vocal chords were still getting used to the lump in my throat that never left after Mama died.

"I can see that from the thrust of your chin and the look in your eye, you are determined. So, I'm going to give you my best advice: get close to the nurse, move in the same circles she does. She'll get so use to seeing you around that after a while, she's bound to slip up. When she does, you'll know what to do."

"What? What will I do?" I questioned.

"That's the tricky part. No one can rightly say."

"What if I don't know what to do?" I protested.

"You will."

"But what if I do the wrong thing?"

"You'll have to work that out if it happens."

I thought a lot about what Mr. Jordan said.

It was the last we ever talked about it. That is, until much later when the whole thing happened.

For the moment, it was all still talk.

CHAPTER NINE

SHOPPING SPREE

"How about skipping out early tomorrow, Bayou," Mr. Jordan asked one spring day.

"I reckon I could. Haven't missed a day of school since Mama passed away and my grades are fairly good. Yeah, sure. Why?"

"We're going to town... that we are," he answered mysteriously.

"What for?"

"Goin' to do a bit of shopping over Monroe while the preacher meets with some people who have burdens over there."

"Great!" I exclaimed. "Not about the people and the burdens... I mean good about going to Monroe."

Mr. Jordan laughed and said, "No need to explain, I know what you mean."

So, the next day we piled in the car with Preacher Wilcox. As I climbed in the backseat, I didn't say so, but I couldn't ever remember riding in a car before this. Maybe I had when I was little, but it must have been a long time ago - a lifetime ago.

I had turned twelve back in February. February the fourteenth, to be exact. Mama always said I was the best Valentine gift she ever got. I never told people when it was my birthday 'cause the older I got, it seemed almost girlie to be born on Valentine's Day. All that red and pink stuff, if you know what I mean. Anyway, I didn't celebrate birthdays nowadays. Don't guess I really ever had.

Every so often on the way to Monroe, the preacher would look back at me and smile. I smiled back and kept on smiling. It sure was nice to be moving, without my too small of shoes pinching my feet each and every step of the way.

Preacher Wilcox talked about planting a garden and how to go about raising enough money to get the sanctuary repainted before Rally Day in the fall. I was kinda surprised to hear him drone on about tedious things like that. I figured preachers only talked about God and heaven – or Satan. Sure didn't think they'd be rambling on about a garden or getting something painted, even if it was the church sanctuary.

Mr. Jordan didn't look surprised so maybe I didn't know as much about preachers as I thought I did. Didn't matter, wasn't planning to be one. When you start telling fibs early, there are some doors that swing shut. More than likely, being a Man of God was one of them.

Still, I did fancy going to church. Somehow, it made me feel like I wasn't poor no more. I really liked learning about Noah and the flood. All those creatures in one boat was something to think about. Just imagine - squirrels next to hunting dogs and chickens next to snakes!

In no time at all, we were gliding up to a parking meter in downtown Monroe. Preacher Wilcox shoved a couple of nickels in the meter and we were off.

I didn't care anything about shopping. Didn't plan on spendin' any of my Story Hour money but I was happy just the same. It was fun to walk down the street, peeking in store windows.

"Come on, Bayou. We've got us some shopping to do and only an hour to get it all done," Mr. Jordan said.

I didn't know whether to speak up or not but as we reached *The Men's Shop*, I decided to confess that I was just along for the ride. "Mr. Jordan, if you don't mind, I'll just look around a bit and meet you back at the car when you're done."

"That won't do. We're here to shop for you."

"Nah, maybe another time. I'm kinda saving my money right now."

I didn't want to be rude, especially since he brought me all the way from Gratis but my Story Hour money had to last me a long, long time - maybe a lifetime.

"Bayou, this shopping trip is on me and my wife. We've been wanting to do something nice for someone for quite a while. The other night we talked about it and we picked you. Juanita is going to be mighty upset if this doesn't turn out right."

"I don't know. The fact that you feed me every Friday night is nice enough. Isn't there anyone else that you'd like to do something for? I think I've about used up my fair share," I said, hopping not to seem ungrateful or unkind.

"Well, that's just it. We thought and we thought... but nobody came to mind – 'cept you. Juanita thought that you would feel this way but I promised her I'd try with all my might."

I didn't say nothin' in return. I was still thinking it all over when he muttered, "She ain't going to like this one little bit. Sure do hate to face her if you refuse. She was countin' on this."

"Well, when you put it that way, I guess so. I wouldn't want her to think that I'm not willing to let her do something nice for someone," I answered.

Truthfully, once it was settled, I was doggone pretty excited 'bout the prospects of something new. I was growing fast and even the clothes from the Caldwells at Christmas were beginning to feel too tight.

Mr. Jordan and I entered in *The Men's Shop* and when it was all over, I walked out with a pair of church pants and new shoes. I felt like a rich kid - the kind you see on television. I couldn't wait until Sunday. I planned on wearing my new stuff every Sabbath - maybe even down the aisle clear to the first pew.

When Mr. Jordan handed me my stuff – in a bag with paper handles, I hugged him right there on the sidewalk, in bright daylight. I didn't care who saw me or what anyone thought.

The ride back was uneventful. Preacher Wilcox talked about the sick and afflicted, how the church needed more land for their cemetery, and who was behind in their giving. I wasn't sure if we were suppose to hear some of the stuff he talked about, but Mr. Jordan acted like it was pretty normal. I sat quiet and listened until the Gratis church steeple came into view.

Then I said, "Preacher Wilcox, would you mind saying a private prayer for a friend of mine?"

"Certainly. And just who may this friend be?"

"Well… not to be rude, sir but I don't really care to say the name," I replied softly. I was still debating whether or not I should say anything at all, but finally decided it was worth the risk.

"A friend of mine has a step-daddy that beats him pretty bad. I sure would appreciate you saying a word to the Father above. At times, I'm not sure how much more my friend can take."

"You can trust me. Strictly confidential."

"I sure appreciate it, sir. But I don't want to bring anymore grief down on my friend, if you know what I mean. And while I'm asking, would you mind asking God to help me get back something that belongs to me?"

"Can you be a little more specific, Son?"

"Well, sir," I answered as Mr. Jordan coughed loudly and slightly shook his head. He was right. I shouldn't have said as much as I did. So, I quickly finished with, "That's about all I can say at the moment."

"Alrighty, then. I'll pray it like you said it. God understands anyway. By the way, come by the church office one day and bring Carl with you. I think I have something that the two of you might be suited to do."

He knows. Why don't the people of this town do something about Carl before something really bad happens?

As if reading my mind, Mr. Jordan said, "Bayou, sometimes things happen that are hard to understand or stop. Interfering in someone else's family is a fine line and tough call."

I knew what he meant. I didn't want anybody poking their nose into my business of living alone.

At least, others were aware of what Carl's step-daddy was doing. I couldn't help feeling a little lighter knowing that the burden of saving Carl didn't rest on my shoulders alone.

For the next couple of weeks, I was so busy taking tests and finishing up the last of my fifth grade history project that I forgot that Preacher Wilcox had something for Carl and me to do. It ended up being a month when Carl and I headed over to the church. Once there, Preacher Wilcox asked us to be his official "bulletin folders".

We agreed.

So, every Sunday morning, we'd arrived at the parsonage and have breakfast with the preacher and his family.

When we finished, we'd head over to the church with Preacher Wilcox and start folding. While he put on his preachin' robe, Carl and I would turn on the lights in all the Sunday School rooms. If the weather was nice, we swing open the windows, too. Last, we'd make a quick pass through the sanctuary just to make sure every pew had hymnals and a bible or two.

After that, we usually hung around. Eventually, we inched our way from the back of the sanctuary to the front. In no time at all, we were sitting dead center every Sunday, smack on the front row.

Preacher Wilcox paid us the first Sunday of every month. But neither Carl nor I felt right about taking money from the church. We even said so, to Preacher Wilcox about it, but he insisted that it was worth every penny to have everything ready for worship when the congregation arrived.

In the end, whenever the collection plate made the rounds, we tried not to let our coins chatter and clank as we gave it all back.

Carl and I figured if anyone got paid for their time and effort, it should be Mrs. Wilcox, the preacher's wife on account of her biscuits.

Carl said, "I've never seen biscuits piled so high or tasted gravy so good. Sunday breakfast makes you want to go right out and get a wife."

"I'd rather starve first," I muttered in reply, licking apple-butter from my chin.

CHAPTER 10

THE NOT SO LAZY DAYS OF SUMMER

The day after school was out for summer, I stopped by to see if Mr. Jordan needed help shutting down the place down. I figured he might feel a tad sad about being away for a couple of months, but when I got there, I found him laughing and strolling around the building with another man.

When Mr. Jordan spotted me, he motioned for me to join them. I did as I was told and made a point of listening to every word they said.

"Mr. Timms, this is the young man that I was telling you about," Mr. Jordan said with a look of pride.

"So, this is Bayou."

"Yes, sir," I said as I offered the stranger my hand.

"Bayou, I'd like for you to meet Mr. Timms. He's the county maintenance supervisor for all the schools."

"Nice to meet you, Mr. Timms," I replied.

"Nice to meet you, too. Mr. Jordan tells me that you're not afraid of work. Is that right?"

"No, sir. I'm not."

Turning back to Mr. Jordan, the man said, "Well

53

then Ed, I trust that the two of you can get the job done. The paint will be delivered in the morning. You know we had to buy in bulk. You're the last school on the list, so any leftover paint is yours to do with - however you see fit. Heck, for all I care, you can paint the trees from here to Monroe. Just don't haul it back to me. I got more leftover stuff in the warehouse than I can ever possibly put to use."

As soon as he left, Mr. Jordan told me that "we" had been hired to paint the school - outside only. Mr. Jordan would be paid two hundred dollars and his assistant would make half of that. Mr. Jordan had picked me for his assistant. I couldn't think. I couldn't speak. *One hundred dollars!* I had already saved closed to twenty from Story Hour. *A hundred dollars! Oh, my stars!*

I wanted to kiss Mr. Jordan - right then and there, for choosing me. But instead I said, "Thank you, kindly, sir" about a hundred times and vowed that I would be the best painter the town of Gratis had ever seen!

Mr. Jordan laughed and said that I might not thank him when it was all said and done 'cause it was one mighty big job.

The very next morning, we started painting. I climbed the ladder and did most of the high work. I never really knew for sure how old Mr. Jordan was, but I was pretty sure that he was getting close to 80. I didn't think he should be up on the ladder. And for once, he seemed inclined to let me do the hard work which I was more than happy to do. It felt good having a purpose and something to do.

After the whole school was painted white as snow, we opened up the trim paint. It was dark green. We painted trim for three straight days until we got it good and right. When we were done, there was still a lot of paint leftover. So, even though we weren't paid to do it, we moved inside the school and painted pretty much everything in there, too.

When that was finished, there were still gallons of paint left. Mr. Jordan laughed and said that instead of painting everything from here to Monroe, he reckoned it would be alright to move on over to his house - which we did.

We painted his house white with dark green trim. It was so white it almost glistened when the evening shadows fell and rays of light sprinkled through the trees on it from the streetlight across the road, or the headlight of a passing car flickered against it. Mrs. Jordan loved it and said it was the prettiest house on the street.

Then, the unthinkable happened. Mr. Jordan suggested that we paint my house, too. At first, I wasn't sure. But finally, he won me over. However, I had one condition. I wanted to do it myself - no help. Reluctantly, he gave in.

My house was little. It only had two bedrooms, a small living room and an even smaller kitchen. I don't know if it had ever been painted before or what the original color had been. I do know at one time the front door had been a lot of different colors. The reason I knew this was the way the paint chipped whenever I went in or out.

When I got ready to paint I discovered we had pretty much run out of white. I had no choice but to paint my house dark green and the trim white.

When it was done, I thought it looked absolutely

wonderful. It had never, ever looked so good, certainly not during all the years Mama and I lived there. It was exciting to live in a freshly painted house. It made me feel proud, even happy. Of course, it made me feel really sad, too. I wish I could have painted the house while Mama was alive. She would have loved living in a freshly painted house. When I mentioned that to Mr. Jordan, he said that it would be a tribute to her if I enjoyed it twice as much; once for her and once for me which made me love him twice as much, too.

CHAPTER ELEVEN

BLOOD BROTHERS

When Mr. Jordan got me the painting job, Carl took over my job out at the Reinquist farm that summer. I recommended him to Mr. Reinquist like Mr. Jordan recommended me to Mr. Timms. It may sound like Carl and I didn't see a lot of each other during the summer months - except for folding bulletins at church, what with my painting job and Story Hour, but nothin' could be further from the truth. We were together more than ever. We were best buddies and blood brothers.

If'n you don't know what a blood brother is, I'll tell you. Both parties take a whittlin' knife and make a small cut in the palm of your hand. Next, you shake hands so that your blood is mixed. Viola – you're blood brothers. It's as simple as that. Anyone can do it. That is, if'n you got a best friend.

Anyway, after work every evening, Carl would swing by my place. At first, we just sat around talking about not much in particular, but as summer wore on, our conversations became more serious.

I knew why Carl came by every evening just before dark. That was when his step-daddy usually got itchy to strike. Carl said his step-daddy slept away his hang-over most of the morning. When he finally did get up, he'd eat a bite and pace the kitchen floor until the sun went down. Then, he'd head back to his favorite barstool over at the Blue Parrot. Next morning, the whole thing would start all over again. Carl said it was during the pacing that he was most likely to get hit or thrown across the room if he chanced to be home then.

I was glad for Carl that his step-daddy had settled down into a regular routine. Once, Carl learned the pattern, it was easy to stay out of the way. It was nice for me, too, because little-by-little Carl's bruises faded away and we were back to wearing short sleeves again.

Carl knew the truth about me, too. He was the only one who knew that every time the door of *The Men's Store* opened over in Monroe the day Mr. Jordan took me shopping, I was searching the face of every man to see if anyone's face resembled mine.

That's the trouble with a lie. When you tell the same one over, you start to believe it yourself. For the life of me, I don't know where I ever got the idea that my daddy and his people lived over near Monroe. But once I got it in my head, it was like the gospel truth. Going to Gratis in the car that day, I wondered what Mr. Jordan and the preacher would have said if they knew they were riding along with a big fat liar in the backseat.

Well, there's only so much barin' of the soul that two boys can do. So, after a couple of heavy-duty talks, Carl and I came up with the idea of runnin' in the evening when the sun started going down. We got the idea after watching the football players at the high school. Not that either of us wanted to play football. We weren't the type that anyone would pick to be on their

58

team, but we figured anyone could run. So, we did.

At first, people sitting on porches or out walking their dogs seemed surprised to see the two of us glide by or around them. We figured out how to go all around the town without doubling back once so after that, we had a regular well-beaten path. After a few weeks of passing the same people time after time, it got so that we spoke-to or joked-with nearly everyone as we went by.

Next thing I knowed, first one or the other person would yell out for us to sit a spell or come on in for a piece of pie. In the end, we ran where there weren't any houses and strolled down the streets that had 'em.

For the first time in my life, I felt like I belonged to everyone and everyone belonged to me. Weird really… but nice. Really nice.

Carl and I always saved the best for last. That way, it worked out so that I got to tell Mr. Jordan and Miss Juanita "good-night" which made for pleasant dreams later when I was home alone.

CHAPTER TWELVE

MRS. PRUITT'S TEETH

The first week in August things went up in smoke. Carl and me had just finished hauling the Jordan's trash out to the street and had no more started for home, when we smelled smoke.

We couldn't tell where it was coming from until we rounded the corner at Maple and Pine. There it was, disaster, in the form of a narrow trail of smoke shooting out the back of Maude Pruitt's house. All of our running paid off because we sprinted and got there in a flash.

Carl ran around to the back of the house in search of a garden hose and I pounded on the door. I could hear Miss Maude shuffling down the hallway. Eventually, her blue hair and shriveled face appeared through a crack in the door. By the way, I don't mean no disrespect by the word "shriveled". It's just that Maude Pruitt turned a hundred-years-old over a year ago, so a "shriveled" face is just a matter of fact.

At the sight of her face, I said, "Miss Maude, your house is on fire. You've got to come with me."

I was ready to help her down the steps just as soon as she took the chain lock off the door and stepped out.

You can imagine my surprise when she said, "I don't gotta go nowhere with you.

Thinking maybe she couldn't hear well or her mind was addled, I repeated, "Miss Maude, your house is on fire. You're got to get out!"

"I don't got to go nowhere if I don't want."

The smoke was getting worse than before and I thought I could actually hear the crackle of fire. "Miss Maude, you don't have a choice. Unchain the door."

I didn't know what I was going to do if the chain didn't come off, but fortunately her trembling fingers unlatched the chain and I stepped in.

"Miss Maude, we gotta go. Here's your cane. I'll help you down the steps. Let's go."

"Boy, you gotta do something for me," she said tearily, looking up at me.

"Yes, ma'am?" I asked, wondering what keepsake or photos she wanted me to get out of the fire.

You can imagine my surprise when she said, "Get my teeth."

"What?"

Be good to people, Bayou.

But Mama…

"My teeth. There in a cup by the bathroom sink. Yonder, down that hallway," Miss Maude said as she pushed me forward.

I pulled my shirt over my nose and mouth.

I bolted down the shadowy hallway.

I found the bathroom but for the life of me, I didn't know if I could actually pick up her teeth. I hesitated but between that and standing there and letting the fire *find* me, I picked up the old lady's choppers.

Now, I don't mind touching frogs, snakes, worms or any manner of things like that, but I sure did feel like I was goin' to pass out and be consumed by flames. Someone's old teeth!

I made my way back down the hallway and out the front door. I could hear the wail of the fire engine but figured it was still a good mile or half away. I hurried over to where Carl had gotten Miss Maude settled in a lawn chair near a tree. She didn't thank me for getting her teeth. Instead, she said, "Now, boy, in the front parlor of my house hangs a portrait of Robert E. Lee. Fetch it to me, boy. Hurry! Run!"

"Ma'am, I don't think I can. Look at the flames shooting out the windows."

"But I want my portrait of Lee. My daddy gave it to me."

"Yes, ma'am, that may be but I can't go back in there." *Teeth are one thing, but a portrait of some dead general is another.*

Then it hit me, for the first time since my mama died, I knew for certain that I didn't want to die, too.

I felt sorry for Miss Maude but I wasn't gonna put my life in danger for any portrait, on anyone's wall.

The question of whether I was, or whether I wasn't going back in, was soon answered.

The roof caved in right over the General. Luckily, by that time, the neighbors had turned out and fire engine number nine was there. Miss Maude was turned over to their care.

Carl and I hung around a bit. Eventually, the fire was out but it wasn't until the following day that I found out how it started from Miss Reader.

"Bayou, Chief Knight told Wiley Duncan… and his wife told me… Miss Maude left the burner on the oven turned on and the window open. Apparently, a breeze caught a dish towel and it landed on the burner. That's what started the whole blaze - an itty bitty dish towel!"

"Really?"

"Yes, I know that you've taken to doing a bit of cooking now and then. You keep this episode in mind, so that the same kind of thing never happens to you."

"Yes, ma'am, I will, but since I don't have no electricity, I doubt that it could happen to me," I answered, without thinking.

"I thought you said that you cooked some grits the other evening. How did you do it - without electricity?"

"Simple, really. A couple of months ago, someone over on Pine threw out an old grill. I knocked on their door and asked if I could have it. Now I use it when I cook. Usually, I just put some twine and branches in the bottom and light a little fire. I also have a couple of pans the Jordans gave me. I fill one half-way up with water. When it's good and hot, I stir in my grits. By that time, the fire is going out, so the grits don't burn if I keep stirring good and hard."

"You're a genius, Bayou. There's not many that could manage the way you have."

"Thank you ma'am."

Not long after that, what started out as Story Hour doughnuts became much more than that. Miss Reader started bringing sausage and biscuits, sometimes ham. I told her that I couldn't eat near that much but she only smiled and said, "Nothing but the best for the best – that's you, Bayou. What we don't eat now, I'll wrap up for you to take home." And she always did.

CHAPTER 13

THE MONEY PROBLEM

I thought that it was going to be a long boring summer. Looking back, it was anything but that. In no time at all, we were all heading back to school. At first, it seemed really strange not to be at the elementary school. It took awhile but I started to like being among older students.

Things were different - better. It didn't seem to matter where I was in the lunch line. I could be at the front of the line, or at the back of the line. The cashier just made a check in her notebook when I said my name. I could pick up a tray - same as those who paid. Sometimes, I felt guilty about being a "free lunch" because of my Story Hour money. I wondered if I should pay regular-like. But then I would start to get worried and nervous just thinking about what could happen if I used up all of my money. What if I had to go to the doctor or hospital or something like that? Who would pay? What would happen to me if I couldn't pay? Would they let me suffer or die? I didn't know the answers to any of that so I decided to keep saying my name when everyone else around me handed the cashier their money. I figured there are worse things than being embarrassed.

Every so often, I'd catch a glimpse of Norma with her tray, laughing and talking with friends. Once or twice, her eyes met mine. No one else could probably understand this, but we were bonded in a weird sort-of-way for life. To this day, I doubt either one of us can eat a peanut-butter sandwich without thinking of each other.

In fact, I'd rather starve than eat another peanut-butter sandwich. Well, maybe I would eat one, if I was on a desert island and it was the only thing to eat. When I'm home, it's mostly bologna on my sandwich now.

Overall, my worries were fewer and had boiled down to these three:

> staying healthy and alive,
> staying out of *The Home*, and
> getting Mama's brooch back.

Make that four:

> finding where they buried Mama.

I pictured her being buried on top of a grassy knoll, under an enormous oak tree. I imagined placing an arrangement of glorious flowers on her grave and having a gentle breeze swirl around me.

First, I had to find her grave. I didn't have a clue how to go about it. Not that I hadn't tried. Carl and I had read every tombstone in the Gratis cemetery but none had Mama's name.

Finally, we gave up looking and I quit talking about it, but I hadn't stopped thinking about it. For now, that's all I could do.

When school started in the fall, I started carrying my money with me. I still had five twenties from painting the school and another twenty-eight dollars from Story Hour. What little I had spent had gone for things like matches, soap powder, bread, bologna, milk and butter.

A new problem popped up. It was a good problem but it was still a worry. If I carried my money with me, I could barely concentrate for worrying about losing my wallet, or someone beating me up and taking it.

If I left my money at home, I worried that someone would break in and take it, although, it would probably be a miracle if someone did find it. It was hidden in a real good spot. I don't 'spect even now I need to tell exactly where it was hidden. No point.

I worried so much, I finally decided to seek expert advice. So, one afternoon I went by the elementary school to talk with Mrs. Caldwell.

"Bayou, you know that I would be more than happy to handle your money for you. You wouldn't have to worry. You could have it back whenever you wanted."

"Yes, ma'am. I know that. I just don't know exactly where I want to keep it. No offense."

"None taken. I understand. Truly, I do. I know how hard you've worked for your money. No one, but no one, deserves it more than you."

"I guess I need to think about it some more."

"Take your time. My offer is always good. Just don't let the money distract you from doing your best in school. I'm counting on you to always do your best."

"Yes, ma'am. I'll try."

I knew that Mrs. Caldwell was honest and good. The only problem being that she was pregnant now. I could just picture some future kid flushing all my money down the toilet or something similar like that. I crossed Mrs. Caldwell off my list of possibilities.

Next, I turned to Mr. Jordan. He said Juanita had been trying all of his life to get him to put their money in the bank. Basically, he had the same problem. I spent so much time with the two of them, I knew where their money was hidden. I reasoned if it wasn't all that hard for me to figure out, it wouldn't be for a robber either.

I crossed the Jordans off my list, too.

Since I didn't want to worry Mr. Jordan, I agreed that putting money in a mason jar and burying it in the ground was a good place. Maybe it was and maybe it wasn't. For me, I didn't want to bury nothin' in the ground again. *Miss you, baby sister.* A sister, almost a year old. Wouldn't that be something!

Saturday rolled around and I still didn't know what to do about the whole money situation.

I decided to talk with Miss Reader before Story Hour to see what she thought I should do.

"Miss Reader, I've got a problem."

"Fire away. I'll help if I can," she answered.

"I've been wondering what to do with my Story Hour money. Doesn't seem safe to leave it at home every day even though I fixed the locks on both doors but I still worry."

"I understand. Have you thought about opening a savings account over at First Main?"

The minute she said it, I knew that was exactly the

thing to do. Wasn't sure how it worked, but a bank sounded safe, a whole lot safer than the toe of Mama's old shoe. Reckon I can tell that now.

"Would they let a twelve-year-old keep their money there? How do you do it? Will it costs me anything?"

"Hold on. Why don't the two of us meet there one afternoon next week when you get out of school. We can work it out. I'll sign for you if you're too young."

"Would you do that, for me?"

"Of course. Now, let's get going. Those little maniacs are going to be bursting through the door any minute, ready to hear their favorite story-reader."

It was settled. We met the following Tuesday afternoon and my money was deposited. I left there with a saving book in my hand, feeling proud and older - like an adult.

Afterwards, *Miss* Reader, who I learned was really a *Mrs.* had her husband and two little girls join us for dinner at Grace's Restaurant.

I had never eaten in a restaurant before this, but I caught on real fast. Afterwards, I wanted to pay for what I ate but the Readers wouldn't hear of it. So, as soon as I got home, I wrote them a note to tell them how much the evening meant to me.

Later that night as I lay in bed listening to night sounds, I thought about what it would be like to eat in restaurants all the time. More than anything else, I thought about what it would be like to have a family.

I had a sister… if only she'd lived.

Yes, a family was definitely worth more than anything money could buy. The whole thing made me

71

think about my savings a little differently. Actually, money could be gotten pretty easily, if you were willing to work hard. Ah... but a family, that's a different matter.

Long toward morning, I slipped out of bed, got down on my knees and prayed, "Dear God, please bless me with a family before I die. Not that I never had one, God. I guess you know that already. It's just that I get so lonely without any relatives at all. I don't mean to complain, really. Just one or two people would do. Amen."

It no time at all, bright sunlight shone through my window - along with Carl's grinning face! In his hand were two homemade fishing poles. I didn't have time to dwell on being lonely any more 'cause fish bite best early morning.

The thought that God had answered my prayer by putting people like Carl in my path flew through my head as I darted out the door.

CHAPTER FOURTEEN

TALKING IT OVER

For some reason, no matter how hard I tried, I couldn't stop thinking about getting Mama's brooch back. It's not like I was going to wear it or anything. It was just one of those things, that no matter how hard you tried, it was always there - just under the surface of everything.

I keep thinking about *that* day. It was like it all happened in slow motion... the hearse... the two men... Mama... silent sobs.

Mainly, I remembered how much the nurse wanted to get away. I'd always heard criminals were anxious to flee the scene of their crime, and the nurse was definitely a criminal in my book. Not only for stealing what was rightfully mine, but for not taking good care of Mama like she was paid to do. No proof really, just my gut feeling. I couldn't bring Mama back, but I was sure gonna' try to get back her brooch.

I didn't know how I was gonna do it, but I knew I needed some kind of plan. I thought of going to the sheriff, but doubted he'd believe me. A couple of times, I thought about getting Carl in on the act. Maybe the two of us could overpower the nurse and just snatch back the brooch, that is - if she happened to be wearing it when we were ready to spring. Otherwise, I'd have to get me another plan.

Of course, I didn't want Satan to snatch my soul for stealing the brooch back. Stealing is stealing, no matter what. But I sure did want Mama's brooch.

I hung around the church a lot, trying to decide what to do. I thought about turning my troubles over to Preacher Wilcox in hopes he could preach a sermon so powerful that the nurse would willingly turn the brooch over to me.

It was hard to make up my mind whether to tell the preacher or not. Got to thinking about how he earned a living. If his entire livelihood came from the congregational giving, then the nurse and maybe even her friends might not put money in the collection plate if they all got crossed up with him. I sure didn't want to put the preacher in a bad spot. In the end, I didn't say anything.

Even so, I was thinking about the brooch more and more. I daydreamed all the time about it. Finally, it got so bad I had to tell myself to put it out of my head and to go on livin'.

Of course, the more I tried not to think about the brooch, the more I thought about it. Mr. Jordan said, "Get on with life or life will roll right over you."

CHAPTER FIFTEEN

ANTICIPATION

Even though, the kids were pretty much the same at the junior high, there were some changes. I now had five teachers instead of one, not to mention all three expected more work in a week than Mrs. Caldwell did in a month. But the biggest difference was there were twice as many of us kids. Busses chugged in from the other side of Gratis with kids from as far as Between, Georgia.

As much as I missed Mrs. Caldwell and Mr. Jordan, I liked being busy. I liked junior high right from the start, especially P.E. class. We climbed long ropes that reached from the ceiling to the floor and we did exercises like Carl's cousin did in the military like push-ups, jumping jacks, squats, all kinds of things.

I also liked social studies. Instead of doing assignments on your own, my teacher, Mrs. Jackson divided the class into groups of four. Sally Roberts, Jerry Knight and Irene Cunningham were on my team. I knew Sally and Jerry from elementary school. Irene lived outside of Between. None of us knew her at first, but she seemed nice enough - for a girl, that is.

Our first assignment was to decide on a team name. We had until Monday to come up with one. Even though we passed notes back and forth during class all week, the four of us could not agree on a single one.

Sally laughed and said, "I don't know about the three of you but I think better when I am out and about, doing something fun."

"Me, too. In fact, I thought up my science fair project while I was shooting hoops with the kid down the street," Jerry added.

"Why don't the four of us meet Saturday afternoon at the soda fountain over in Monroe," Sally suggested.

"I didn't know there was a soda fountain in Monroe," Jerry said with a puzzled look.

"It's in the back of the drugstore on Main Street," Irene said and then added, "Let's meet for lunch, say around twelve o'clock?"

"Sounds good to me," I answered. Of course, I would have to check with Mrs. Reader but I was pretty confident that she could spare me come Saturday morning.

"Great! They have the best hot dogs east of the Mississippi," Irene stated matter-of-fact like.

"And ice cream sundaes to die for. I can hardly wait," Sally added.

"It's settled then. Saturday. Be there or be square," Jerry said with a laugh.

As soon as the girls headed off, Jerry said to me, "Meet me early Saturday morning out at the Reinquist farm. Transportation is on me."

I couldn't believe it. I thought for sure that I would have to start walking before daybreak to make it there.

"Are you sure, Jerry. I mean if it's any trouble, I can get there on my own."

"Don't thank me now. Wait and see," he answered mysteriously.

Although I tried to get him to tell me more, that's all he would say before we parted and he went one way and I went another.

I made my way over to the elementary school to help Mr. Jordan. He'd cleaned half of the building and was just about to start on what use to be mine when I arrived. I could hardly work for talking. I was so excited about tomorrow. *I'll get my own milkshake and French fries, Daddy.*

Finally, we finished. Mr. Jordan understood about me not going home with him for our usual Friday evening supper. I hated missing but I needed to get to the library before closing time. Mrs. Reader was shelving the last returns of the day when I arrived. I pitched in and we got them done in no time at all.

As we were leaving, I cleared my throat and said, "Mrs. Reader, something has come up and I'm afraid that I won't be able to do Story Hour like usual."

"Is anything the matter? You're not sick are you?"

"No ma'am. It's just that my Social Studies group from school is meeting to choose a team name. We made plans to meet tomorrow in Monroe."

"I see. May I ask a question?"

"Sure."

"Why Monroe instead of here in Gratis?"

"Well, Irene Cunningham said the soda fountain there has the best hot dogs east of the Mississippi and Sally Roberts said that the ice-cream sundaes are to die for," I blurted out.

"Then by all means, I think you should go. I do have one favor to ask."

"Yes ma'am," I answered, wondering if she wanted me to do something around the library when I got back.

"I want you to eat enough for the two of us," she answered with a laugh.

"Yes, ma'am, I will. I truly will," I said happily as we locked the library door and went down the steps.

"And Bayou, don't go thinking that you can skip out any old time you want. I need you and the kids love you. You are so kind and good with them. Everyone says so, you know."

"Thanks, Mrs. Reader."

This may sound stupid, but I couldn't help thinking that I needed them just as much as they needed me. And I did.

I could have done without *Story Hour with Moms* and *Story Hour with Dad*. That's when parents are invited to share their favorite childhood book with the group. That was hard. It made me long for Mama, but all of the other times weren't bad by a long shot.

Sometimes I'd pretend that I was reading a fairy tale to my little sister instead of a child I barely knew. But as time went by, I thought about Mama and my baby sister less and I was glad about that.

Sometimes, you just gotta go on, no matter what if you don't want life to roll right over you.

CHAPTER SIXTEEN

BECOMING A RISK-TAKER

I jumped out of bed Saturday morning and in no time at all, made it over to the Reinquist farm. Even though I was excited about going to Monroe with friends, I couldn't imagine why Jerry wanted me to meet him at the Reinquists until I got there.

Although, I had worked summers there, I'd forgotten that Mrs. Reinquist was Jerry's mother's cousin. It seems Jerry had promised to pick up a load of seeds in Monroe for the use of their old tractor. So, we hooked up an old hay wagon on the back and started down the road.

The first couple of miles, I sat on the back of the wagon, my feet swinging freely in the air. Eventually, I got tired of looking at the scenery and shouted at Jerry to stop. I jumped on the tractor hitch and gripped the edge of his metal seat. Even though the tractor was loud, at least we could shout back and forth a bit.

When we came to the creek, we both jumped off. We rolled our trousers up and took off our shoes. We waded in the creek, splashing and laughing, careful not to get too messed up. We knew the girls wouldn't like it if we arrived dirty.

Once we got goin' again, it didn't take long to get to the highway. We rode on the shoulder of the road when there was a car and bounced back on the highway when no one was in sight.

Finally, we were on the outskirts of Monroe. Jerry pulled the tractor behind *Best Seed and Feed* and we hopped inside.

"May I help you?" a clerk asked.

"Yes, but it may be a little while. We are here to pick up a seed order for the Reinquists over in Gratis," Jerry answered with a grin.

"I've already put it on their bill. Do you need someone to help you carry them out?"

"Well, we've got another stop to make while we're here. Is it alright to leave our tractor around back until we're through?" Jerry questioned.

"Sure. Just let me know when you're ready and we'll get the bags of seeds loaded on the wagon."

"Thanks. We'll be back," Jerry answered as we turned to go.

We crossed the street and headed toward the Drugstore. I wasn't surprised to see that the girls were already there. They were waiting for us out front.

"Hey everybody," Jerry yelled.

"Was that you driving a tractor? Our car passed a tractor several miles back, but I wasn't sure," Irene said.

"Sure was," Jerry answered.

"I just knew that was you," Sally said to me.

"Did you see my white knuckles? I was hanging on for dear life," I said making light of our pokey mode of transportation.

"Hey, we got here, didn't we?" Jerry answered

with a laugh and then added, "Just you wait until I get a car. You'll all be beggin' me to haul you from place to place."

We laughed some more as we found a seat at the counter. As soon as our food came, we got down to the business of deciding on a name for our team. We took turns saying whatever popped in our mind. Irene wrote them all down. After much discussion, we narrowed it down to two: *First in the Class* and *Risk Takers*. The girls like *First in the Class* and Jerry and I like *Risk Takers*. No matter how many times we voted, it always ended up two votes for each.

A man sitting at the counter leaned over and whispered something in Irene's ear. She looked surprised. Then, she smiled and whispered something to Sally. Sally looked surprised and then she, too, smiled. Then Irene suggested we vote one more time. This time, it was 4 - 0.

"Yeah! *Risk Takers* it is," Jerry said triumphantly.

"Suits me," I answered.

I turned to thank the stranger but he was gone.

CHAPTER SEVENTEEN

SNAP DECISION

Mrs. Jackson was turning out to be my second favorite teacher. Mrs. Caldwell being the first, of course. I loved being one of the *Risk Takers*. It was like belonging to a secret club or something. I liked feeling like I belonged somewhere. The more work Mrs. Jackson poured on, the better I liked it.

In the beginning, we worked at school in the afternoons. Later, we began meeting in the library after everyone had a chance to go home to eat and get back. As for me, there wasn't any reason to go home first, so I would hang around the library helping Mrs. Reader until the rest of the *Risk Takers* got there. When I wasn't doing Story Hour, Mrs. Reader sent me to the basement to file and sort old newspaper clippings about local events.

I loved the stillness of the library basement. Sometimes, I played music on the radio while I worked. There were several long tables and comfortable chairs. There was even an old sofa. Often, I spent the night there.

Mrs. Reader told me, "That's perfectly fine. Not a living soul is going to mind." The best part about sleeping there was whenever I had trouble falling asleep, I'd just go upstairs to get a good book to read.

During the last week of April, Irene Cunningham said, "We're not going to get through with our social studies project if we don't start spending more time on it. I think we're going to have to give up fun stuff on weekends, at least until we get all of the paper strips torn and ready to make the papier-mache."

"What about you, Jerry? Are you free Sunday afternoon?" Sally questioned.

"Sure. I want to be the one who gets to shape the volcano out of that paper-whatever it is," Jerry answered.

"Papier-mache. What about you, Bayou?" Sally asked.

"Sure, no problem," I answered happily. Sundays were long and boring. I'd be happy to have some place to go after church.

"Then, it's settled," Irene said. "Be at my house this coming Sunday around 1:00. Don't forget to bring crayons. We've got a lot of landforms to draw before we can even think about building a volcano."

Both girls turned to go one way and Jerry and I peeled off in the other direction. All of a sudden, it hit me that I didn't know where Irene lived.

"No problem," Jerry laughed. "I've got directions. Meet me in front of the library. It's on the way."

"I'll be there, crayons and all," I answered, in a singsong voice, like a girl.

"You're crazy, Bayou Brown, crazy," Jerry said before disappearing through Maude Pruitt's back hedge and darting across her lawn to take a shortcut home.

I went in search of Carl. That was the only thing

that I didn't like about being a *Risk Taker*. I wasn't spending much time with Carl but he was busy working on his team project with the *Academic A's*. He hated their name but loved working with Marsha Bennett, the cutest girl in seventh grade.

I guess everything has a price.

CHAPTER EIGHTEEN

AT WHAT COST?

The next couple of days flew by and in no time at all, Jerry and I were ringing Irene's doorbell.

"Come on in," said a familiar throaty adult voice I couldn't quite place.

Jerry bounded in and I followed. Immediately, I was aware of the odor of cigarettes but before I even had time to think clearly, Irene appeared and motioned for the two of us to follow her.

Sally was already working when we entered the kitchen. "Hey, guys. Glad you're here. We've got a lot to do. Pull up a chair and get started."

"Fine with me. Don't want to be here all day," Jerry answered as if he had other, more important things to do.

"Bayou, why don't you tear strips of paper? Once Irene and Jerry get the cardboard volcano in place, we can start putting on the papier-mache. I'll get the water and glue mixed up."

"Okay," I muttered, ripping strips of newspaper, all the while wiping sweat from my forehead.

About that time, a voice from the hallway called, "Irene, I'm runnin' an errand. "I'll be back in ten minutes."

"Sure, mom. No problem," Irene answered as she glued the base of the volcano to the cardboard.

Eventually, the volcano was ready. The four of us started dipping strips of paper in the glue mixture and wrapping the volcano with strip-after-strip of gooey newspaper until we ran into a problem. We were running out of paper strips faster than we were making it up the side of the volcano.

Irene suggested that I go to her mom's room and get a pair of scissors out of her mother's sewing basket on her dresser. That way, I could cut through several layers of newspaper at one time, producing paper strips faster.

"Great idea," I called as I darted up the stairs for the scissors. I didn't have any trouble finding them and was just about to leave her mother's bedroom when I saw *it*. The brooch! Mama's brooch!

My breathing was so jagged. I felt dizzy and wondered briefly if I was dying. I bent over and put my head between my knees for a couple of minutes. I looked toward the stairs and back down at the brooch. Then I wrapped my fingers tightly around the brooch and stuffed it deep into my pocket before starting slowly back down the stairs.

"What took you so long," Irene questioned.

"I had trouble finding the sewing box," I answered. *Another lie.*

"Come on, man, get busy before the glue dries," Jerry said with a playful punch to my shoulder.

I wanted to run out the door and never come back. My heart said, "Go! Go! Go now!" But my head was telling me to stay. I didn't want to draw any attention to myself. So, I stayed.

About the time we got the paper strips and glue to the top of the volcano, Irene's mother walked in the kitchen. It *was* her. The nurse. The thief.

"Hey mom, come and see our volcano. It's a prop for our Hawaii project," Irene said proudly.

"I see. It looks interesting but have you forgotten your manners young lady?" Mrs. Cunningham questioned.

"I'm sorry. This is Jerry and this is Bayou. You already know Sally," Irene said while putting on the last of the glue mixture.

"Nice to meet you both," Mrs. Cunningham said staring at me.

"Nice to meet you, ma'am," I mumbled.

"Don't I know you from somewhere?" Mrs. Cunningham questioned with a puzzled expression on her face.

"I don't know. I don't think so," I answered, trying not to give myself away. *More lies.*

"Hummm," she said as she walked to leave the room.

The four of us did a quick clean-up and I made a hasty exit. I needed to think. I needed a plan. But what I really needed was Mama. Of course, that could never be.

The thought of going home to an empty house was more than I could bear. So I headed to the library. It was closed but Mrs. Reader had given me a key. There wouldn't be anyone there on a Sunday evening so I could be alone to think.

As I lay on the old sofa in the cool basement of

the library, I remembered something Mr. Jordan told me a long time ago, "sometimes no action is action."

The more I thought about it, the more I decided to do nothing 'cept hold onto Mama's brooch which I did throughout the night.

CHAPTER NINETEEN

ONLY A MATTER OF TIME

For the next couple of days, I tried to remain calm.

Every time I wrapped my fingers around Mama's brooch, I felt secure.

At first, I tried to think of a safe place to hide it, but in the end, I couldn't part with not having it near me. So, I kept it in my pant's pocket with a couple of quarters and my pocket knife. It seemed like the perfect place, if for no other reason - no one could steal it back without me knowin' it.

I did have one close call. One evening when Carl and I were running, I jumped up over the Reinquist fence and hit the ground with such force that two quarters flew out of my pocket. Luckily, Mama's brooch stayed put.

I tried to be more careful. Even though Carl was my best friend in the whole wide world, I didn't want to put him in the position of knowin' about the brooch, in case either of us were hauled in for questioning. I wasn't sure exactly sure about the law, but figured knowing about a criminal act couldn't be good. So, I was determined to keep Carl out of it… if I possibly could.

Three days went by. I reasoned - the more days, the better. Maybe other people would be in-and-out of the Cunningham house and it wouldn't be tracked back to me. I couldn't have been more wrong.

Just before school was out the following Monday afternoon, Mr. Moore, the principal showed up at my classroom door. Behind him in the doorway stood a police officer I didn't recognize. Mrs. Jackson said for the class to keep on working and went out to talk with them.

When she returned, she said, "Bayou Brown, Mr. Moore would like to see you."

"Yes ma'am."

You could hear a pin drop when I stood up. My legs were trembling. I wondered if I could make it over to where they were waiting.

Mrs. Jackson continued, "Bayou, you won't be coming back today so gather your things, dear." Now, instead of looking at me, everyone looked down. It's bad enough when teachers call you by both names but when they tell you to pack up your stuff, it's beyond bad. Everyone knows that, even if they don't know why.

"Yes ma'am." *Worse than I thought. Not coming back today or ever? I didn't know how long of a jail term I was likely to get, but I doubted I'd make it back before algebra, and that was still a couple of years away.*

As I got close enough to read the officer's badge, I knew for certain I wouldn't be back for algebra, much less ever see the light of day again. There was no mistaking the block letters that spelled out his name: Officer Cunningham.

CHAPTER TWENTY

IN THE LINE OF DUTY

"Son, my sister says that you took something that belonged to her, is that right? What have you got to say for yourself?"

"Nothin' sir," I answered.

"Well, nothin' is not goin' to cut it, understand?"

"Yes sir. I understand sir."

"Where are your parents? We might want to call and get them down here," Officer Cunningham said with more force and a tad of spit.

"Don't got none," I replied, never looking up.

"Don't lie to me. You've got parents or you wouldn't be here. You'd be over at *The Home for the Needy*, now wouldn't you?"

After that comment, Mr. Moore spoke up, "Officer, Bayou here, lost his mother a year or two ago."

"Well, then who are his guardians, that's what I'd like to know," the officer answered gruffly.

"You'll have to ask him. I'm not rightly sure."

"Do you mean to tell me that you have no records or files to check? I need that information before I can proceed with this. My sister is very angry. She loved that brooch and aims to have it back."

"I'm on my own and she's not getting' it back," I blurted without thinking.

"Then, you are admitting that you stole it, is that right?"

"No, sir. You can't steal what's yours to begin with," I answered looking straight ahead.

"Well, we'll just see about that. You're coming with me. I have some phone calls to make." He grabbed my arm and jerked me down the hall and out to the patrol car. Once there, he shoved me in the back.

In no time flat, we were at the fire station where Gratis policemen work out of a couple of rooms in the back. Opposite a tiny bathroom, was a holding cell. It was smaller than a closet and only had enough room for a cot and tin pan. I gathered from the lingering stench, the pan was the bathroom.

I fell on the cot and stared at the ceiling. Officer Cunningham made several phone calls but I didn't even bother to listen. No one was going to come to my aid. No one was going to bail out the poorest kid in town. My life was pretty much over by all accounts, no doubt. And for the moment, I really didn't care.

I guess I was worn out from the whole ordeal because I must have slept for an hour or two. The next thing I remember was Officer Cunningham saying, "Bayou, you've got to stay here for the night. In the morning, a judge will listen to your case and decide where you'll be sent after that. I'll be back in the morning to fetch you. Good night." *Good night. Was that something policemen say just to lull you into thinking you're safe?*

There wasn't anything "good" about this night that I could see. I'd blown it. I didn't make it after all.

What a pity. What a waste. Wondered what Mr. Jordan and Mrs. Reader would say. I wondered if Preacher Wilcox would use me as the example of what not to do. Hated to think what Mrs. Caldwell would have to say. And Carl. I hoped he wouldn't feel too bad knowing he had been best friends with a common crook. Nothin' would ever be the same again - all on account of me. Guess I was in the right group after all. Risk Takers. That's me, for sure. Unfortunately!

CHAPTER TWENTY ONE

JAILHOUSE BLUES

Now, I don't scare easy but when the lights all went out 'cept for one at the other end of a dim hallway, I started to feel uneasy. To top it off, I kept hearing the kind of scratching sound an animal would make. I looked around but didn't see anything until a grinning face bobbed behind the bars in a small window near the ceiling in my cell. My spirits soared as I dashed toward the window.

"Carl!"

"Hey, buddy."

"Carl, I've really messed up. Once you hear what I've done, you'll never want to be friends with me again," I said with deep regret. Carl deserved better than this.

"You know better than that," he answered.

"How did you know where to find me?" I wondered aloud.

"Not hard. Visited my step-daddy here a time or two. Mama made me. Always hoped those dense cops would notice the bruises all over me and lock him up for life, but of course, they never did.

"I know," I answered sadly.

"Hey, the window will open a bit if you push on

the bottom right," he said with authority. I climbed up on the bed and helped pry open the window from inside.

"Here," Carl said as he tossed a wad of wax paper my way.

"What the heck?" I questioned.

"Leftover fried chicken."

"Thanks," I said, trying hard not to cry.

"Thought you might have missed dinner."

"Carl, I've really messed up this time."

"Maybe, maybe not. What happened?"

Like water over a dam, words tumbled from my mouth. I told him everything from "a" to "z", everything about missing Mama, burying the baby girl and the brooch - everything. Then I bawled.

Carl never said a word. Just hung onto the windowsill halfway up the building as I poured out my heart. Then, he cried too. I think we were crying for each other, really. When we were through, we looked at each other and grinned. We did that sometimes, just knowing we had each other.

"Go on home, now. I'm fine. Whatever happens, I'd do it all the same again."

"See y'a buddy," Carl said as he slid off the windowsill and down to the ground.

"See y'a Carl," I answered to the night sky, wondering if I ever would.

CHAPTER TWENTY-TWO

LIES, LIES AND MORE LIES

Early the next morning, Officer Cunningham came back. He brought me a wash cloth and a toothbrush. As he unlocked my cell he said, "Go down the hall and get cleaned up a bit."

"Yes sir," I answered.

"And don't look so worried. It's not like you took a life or anything."

"I won't, sir. You're right, sir," I replied, feeling somewhat better.

His wife showed-up around nine o'clock with toast and bacon. A couple of the firemen came in and everyone sat around talking about the weather and things like what kinds of tomato seeds grew best. I never said nothin'.

The bright spot of the morning was when Officer Cunningham's wife rose to leave. She patted me on the shoulder and said, "Don't worry. Things usually turn out all right."

I wasn't so sure but it felt nice to have the hand of a mother pat your shoulder. I figured it might be my last human contact for quite a long time.

Finally, we walked to the patrol car but this time,

Officer Cunningham said I could sit up front.

"We're going to the courthouse over in Monroe."

"Will people from *The Home* be there?"

"Probably. They provide a lot of social services to a lot of people for a wide variety of reasons," he answered.

As we drove up, I saw Irene Cunningham and her mother. Irene looked shocked. Her mother looked mad.

"Probably mad 'cause I don't have you in handcuffs and chains," Officer Cunningham muttered, seemingly more to himself than me.

Mrs. Cunningham motioned for her brother to roll down the car window before we came to a complete stop. "Al, I hope this isn't an indication of whose side you're on."

"No one's on any side, Ailene. Seems to me, being a nurse, you'd have an ounce of compassion in you somewhere," the officer answered.

"You're my brother, no matter what. You'd better remember that here today," Mrs. Cunningham said as she crossed the parking lot and swept ahead of us, dragging Irene behind her.

"I'm not likely to forget it," he answered and then whispered, "Oh, if I only could."

I wanted to laugh but didn't. Besides, as Mr. Jordan always said "Talk is cheap. Now, actions - that be another matter."

As we entered the large conference room, I felt scared. I never looked up. I just followed the shoes of Officer Cunningham until I sat down and looked up at an important looking elderly man. *Ah, the judge.* So, he's the one who will decide my fate. The one with the power to send me back where I belong or turn me over to *The Home*. Which one will it be? Does it really matter? No one's waiting for me at either place. Well, of course it matters. I want to go home.

The judge banged his gavel. "Most irregular. People, we're running out of seating room. Some of you are going to have to stand and if you're going to stay, you're going to have to be quiet."

There was a lot of shuffling, several coughs and a lot of whispering. I figured a lot of people had to look at you when they were determining where to send you. I wrapped my fingers around Mama's brooch - still in my pocket, tighter than ever.

After a lot of scraping of chairs, the judge said, "You'll get your turn. However, in order to be fair, I need to hear from Ailene Cunningham and her daughter, Irene first.

A click of heels proceeded Mrs. Cunningham's voice. "Well, sir. I can hardly believe after all that I've done for this boy, that I would even be here today."

"Start at the beginning, Mrs. Cunningham. I want to hear it all even if it takes us all day."

"Thank you, kindly sir. I was assigned the privilege of taking care of his mother after the birth of her son... uh daughter... uh baby...whatever. Anyway, I went way out there to see her every single week, sometimes more. Lovely soul really. I did all that I could. In fact, I would even stay over so that I could talk to Bayou and make sure that he was doing all right."

At that point, she stopped to take a hankie out of her purse.

Mrs. Cunningham dabbed her eyes a couple of

101

times as if she was going to burst into tears any moment, which I suspected she was not.

The judge looked concerned and said, "Mrs. Cunningham, would you like a glass of water before going on?"

"Yes, sir. The mere thought that I should be repaid in such a manner is sometimes more than I can bear."

After Mrs. Cunningham was given a glass of water, the judge said, "Please continue."

"Well, sir, my daughter Irene was kind enough to invite this young man over to work on a school project, along with some other classmates. I left to run a quick errand and apparently, he dashed upstairs and stole my brooch."

"Okay, let's hear from your daughter."

Irene walked by me and took the chair at the front that her mother was now leaving.

The judge continued, "Can you confirm what your mother has told us?"

"It's true, I guess. Bayou went upstairs for scissors and the next thing I knew, Mother was back and the brooch was missing," Irene said softly.

"Thank you. I guess we need to hear from you now, Bob Brown."

"Bayou," I said without thinking.

"What did you say?" The judge sounded aggravated.

"My name is Bayou, not Bob," I replied softly.

"I stand corrected. Anyway, is this the truth of the matter? Think before answering. Although, you are not under oath, I expect to hear the truth, young man.

There's nothing to be gained from a lie."

Before I could answer, voices behind said "I did it", "I'm the one", "Blame me", and "I took the brooch".

I whirled around. For the first time, I realized standing behind me was nearly every person I've ever known in my entire life; Mrs. Caldwell, Mrs. Jackson, the Jordans, Preacher Wilcox, the Reinquists, Jerry, Sally, Mrs. Reader, some of the kids from Story Hour, Maude Pruitt in a wheelchair and in the middle of it all, sat Carl with a huge grin on his face.

"Order! Order! You'll all get to talk but I can't hear anyone unless everyone talks one at a time," the judge said sharply. Then he looked back at me, "Seems like you're mighty special, kid."

I tried to answer but words wouldn't come out of my mouth so I put my head down on the table and cried. It probably sounds like I am some big crybaby or something, and maybe I am. But when you've had a miserable childhood or been abused as a kid like Carl, when someone is nice to you, there's not a lot you can do to control your feelings, no matter how hard you try.

For the next hour or so, I only heard bits and pieces. Things like Mrs. Caldwell saying, "I took the brooch. I shouldn't have I know, especially when I consider how much Bayou taught me about honesty. You see, he was in and out of my room a lot in the afternoons. I never had reason or cause, to lock-up my purse. He could have taken my money anytime he wanted but he didn't. What makes this even more remarkable is the fact that Bayou didn't have money or anything much. It's easy to do right when you have everything, don't you think? A bit harder when you don't."

The kids from Story Hour talked about how much they like hearing me read and having me help them pick out books. One little girl even said, "If I had a big brother, I'd want it to be Bayou."

I heard Preacher Wilcox say that I handled the collection plates many a day and never once was one cent missing.

Mrs. Cunningham's answer to that was "How would you know, if the money wasn't counted yet? How would you know really? Maybe he's been stealing from the church and you're just too blind to know it."

Preacher Wilcox laughed and said, "Nope. Not the case. The church offering has continued to swell and grow. Maybe I'm a better preacher than I thought if he's been skimming off the top."

That got a hearty laugh.

As for me, I felt outraged that anyone would think that I would steal from the church. Just the thought of it made me really mad, until I caught Sally's eye and she winked. So, I tried to laugh along with everyone else instead.

"I took the brooch," Mr. Reinquist said. "Crops not doing good. I should have known better because Bayou taught me to work hard and not take the easy way out like some in the area that went bankrupt around here. Bayou never once cheated by picking up wormy apples off the ground instead of hauling ladders and climbing to the top for the good ones. He could have, you know. He sure could have."

Then, Mrs. Jackson said, "It was me. I took the

brooch. I wanted something nice to wear. Teachers don't make much and I just wanted it. Thought I would wear it whenever I go out of town. No one would know. Shouldn't have, but teachers are human, too."

I knew no one would believe her. She didn't have the look of someone who would steal. Besides, everyone knows teachers don't steal.

"I took it. I wanted a gift for my wife. I'm an old man. Throw me in the clinker for the rest of my life, but let this boy go home where he belongs. No, I shouldn't have taken it. Bayou was the one who taught me to do for others. He stayed day-after-day to help me, an old janitor, get through with my work early so that I could go home and have dinner with my wife. He did it for free, too. Send me to jail in place of him,"
Mr. Jordan said in a loud voice.

"Why, Mr. Jordan, how dare you! You know good and well you didn't take the brooch because it wasn't there to take. I took it," Maude Pruitt said in her old, screechy voice as she wheeled closer to the front of the room.

"And just how did you get your wheelchair up the stairs at the Cunningham house, may I ask?," Mr. Jordan asked.

"You've got me there," Maude answered.

Everyone laughed. Then she started again, "Just let me say this. I may be old. I may look like a sweet little old lady but I tell you now, I AM NOT! I wanted that brooch so badly, I crawled every step of the way. Once there, I used my cane to swipe it off of the dresser. Of course, I couldn't get around in my own house when it caught on fire. In fact, I was too upset to find my cane and wouldn't have made it out alive if not for Bayou and that other boy, what's his name?"

"Me, Carl," Carl answered, as he shot straight up in the air from his chair. "But Miss Maude, you know good and well, you never took that brooch. I did and I did it for Bayou. You see, he's been more than a brother to me. I 'spect most of you already know that my step-daddy beats me morning, noon and night. I'd probably be dead now if I didn't have Bayou's to run to in the middle of the night."

With that, a gasp went around the room.

Carl continued, "I can't wear short sleeves, even in the middle of the summer. But what you don't know is, Bayou won't go sleeveless either - on account of supporting me."

Carl looked at me and nodded as if to say "It's okay. Everything is out in the open now and I don't care.

Then he continued, "So, when I knew he wanted the brooch back, I was determined to help him get it, one way or another. And I did just that."

Things went on-and-on like that for another thirty minutes or so. For a second or two, I even thought that Officer Cunningham was going to get up and claim to be a thief, too.

Until that day, I'd forgotten the ending of Mama's words "...*and they'll be good to you.*"

Suddenly, Mrs. Reader exclaimed, "Oh, my goodness, I completely forgot. I've got proof that the brooch belongs to Bayou."

Everything came to a halt – everything; taping feet, a soft cough or two, the shuffling of papers, even the jingle of coins in Preacher Wilcox's pocket.

Sternly, the judge said, "Mrs. Reader, is it? I've heard enough exaggerations and lies. In the interest of this young man, if you do indeed have positive proof, come forward please."

Mrs. Reader started to dig in her enormous black leather purse, her face buried beneath her wild red hair as she dug deeper and deeper. In the end, she had to dump the entire contents on the long table. Things scattered everywhere as her polished red nails flittered through it all. Finally, she pulled up a torn and yellowed piece of newspaper.

"See... right here!" she exclaimed as she hurriedly smoothed out a picture of five women standing on the steps of the church and flashed it toward the judge. The caption under the picture read "Gratis Volunteers Cook for Visiting Missionaries".

A gasp from Ailene Cunningham escaped just as the room exploded into thunderous applause.

I slid the brooch from my pocket and lay it on the table in front of the judge.

Finally, the judge spoke, "Well, this concludes our investigation. Bayou, I'd like to talk with you privately in my office for a few minutes."

"Yes sir," I answered as I stood up and followed him into his office. I was hoping he'd call Mrs. Reader back, too, so I could get a better look at the picture but he didn't.

Once the judge removed his robe and we were seated in his office, he said, "Young man, what I've witnessed here is something I'm not likely to see again. I want to know more about you and your family."

"I have no family."

"Is there an aunt or grandmother or someone that checks on you? Anyone?"

"No sir, I'm all there is."

"My notes say here that you are only twelve-years-old. Is this right?"

"No sir, I'm thirteen now. Been thirteen for a couple of months."

"Where do you live?"

"Where I've always lived. My granddaddy gave the house to Mama and me."

"But... but... who takes care of you?"

"I guess I do."

"But isn't that awfully hard?"

"Sometimes... but in a way - everyone takes care of me."

"Exactly what do you mean by that?"

"Well, Mr. and Mrs. Jordan make sure that I have a good meal every Friday night. And they give me tons of leftovers that last all weekend. Mrs. Reader hired me to read to the little ones at Story Hour every Saturday and that pays two dollars a week. Mr. Timms hired me to paint the school and paid me one hundred dollars. Mrs. Caldwell makes sure that I have school supplies and still leaves food in the boiler room for me and other stuff, too. Maude Pruitt hires me to mow her lawn in the summertime. Preacher Wilcox hired me and Carl to fold bulletins and he pays us, but we don't take the money due to it being church work and all. Someone offered to buy my lunch every day but I said no 'cause that would leave Norma Baker the only free lunch. Sometimes..."

"Whoa. Are you telling me that you are being raised by the entire community?"

"Yes, sir, I guess I am."

"I have never in my life heard of such a thing."

"Gratis people are good people."

The judge nodded. "But do you ever get lonely?"

"Sometimes, but not that much. Carl and I hang out together and we run around Gratis a lot. Well, really we're out talking to people more than running."

"Sounds to me like you are doing a great job on your own. However, I would love to take you over to *The Home for the Needy*. Now, I know that it may not be the place for everyone but it's really not as bad as you might think. You could stay there until you turn eighteen. They feed you good and you always have people around you. There's quite a few kids living there now. What do you say?"

"Sir, I really don't think that it would be for me."

"May I ask what makes you so sure?"

"Well, there may be people around me but it wouldn't be my people: Mrs. Caldwell, Mr. Jordan, Mrs. Reader, Carl and all the others."

"I understand but don't rule it completely out. In fact, I'm ordering you to show up here one day next week so that you and I can take a tour. No reason not to do that. Then, if you still want to go it on your own, that's fine. What do you say?"

I didn't want to do it, but didn't feel like I could refuse so I merely answered, "Fine, I'll be back."

The judge held out his hand. "Promise?"

"I promise," I answered as the two of us shook hands.

For the next couple of days, I thought of little else. At times, I almost thought that it would be good to not be the one in charge, not to have the worry of making it from day to the next.

I talked about it Friday evening with the Jordans. Mr. Jordan said, "Bayou, lookin's cheap. Go, take the tour. You'll never know whether it's the right thing or not, if you don't face it squarely in the eye. Besides, you shook the man's hand and you know you can't go back on that."

"I guess you're right. It's just that I've spent the last couple of years trying not to go there. Seems funny to be going there of my own free will, if you know what I mean."

"I do. It was like that for my people when slavery ended. They spent their lives wantin' their freedom, then when it came, it was hard to know which way to turn, 'specially, since they never really expected it and weren't able to prepare for it in advance."

"What did they do?"

"Some took off and some stayed right where they were. Imagine that."

"I think I understand. Hard to know which way to turn," I said as I gave him a big hug.

After we pulled apart, Mr. Jordan tapped his heart and said, "No matter where you are, you'll always be in my heart."

"I know. You, too, always." I answered as I looked back at the face I dearly loved and the man who was never the one to quit hugging first which always meant the world to me.

If I had known what would happen next, I'd never have left.

Mr. Jordan died peacefully in his sleep that night.

Mrs. Jordan arrived at my house early the next morning to fetch me to help out. She wanted me by her side as she made funeral arrangements, saying "I 'spect we were the two who loved him the most."

Looking back, it's strange really. I felt such a peace about losing Mr. Jordan and so did Mrs. Jordan.

She said, "You know, Bayou, he was old. It was his time to go and we had such a good life. Never a cross word between us. Not once. How many people can say that?"

"Very, very few," I answered, thinking that was what I wanted when it came time to choose a wife. Of course, that was a long way off. For now, I kept my thought to myself and helped Mrs. Jordan all that I could.

From that time on, I did the mowing and odd jobs around the house for her. I was always there when something needed to be fixed or painted.

I've never stopped missing Mr. Jordan. Probably never will.

Once when we were cleaning their shed out back, she told me that he said that I had been a better son to him than his own flesh and blood. I never knew until that moment, they had a son.

I had questions but Mrs. Jordan wasn't too inclined to talk about him, other than to say that he left home because he was ashamed his dad was a janitor and he hadn't been back since.

CHAPTER TWENTY-THREE

THE HOME, FINAL DECISION

I didn't get back to the judge the following week like I promised but once I explained about Mr. Jordan, he said that he understood and that it was alright. He suggested we visit *The Home* the following Saturday.

The week flew past and in no time at all, the two of us were walking up the driveway of *The Home*. The large white house looked like it should be on the cover of a magazine.

Once inside, we were greeted by a Catholic nun and a bunch of laughing, grinning boys and girls on their way outside to have a picnic under enormous shady trees on the front lawn. I immediately noticed a large cardboard box full of fried chicken and steaming ears of corn-on-the-cob. The sight of it all made me realize that I hadn't eaten all day.

As if reading my mind, the nun motioned for us to join them, saying, "It's not every day we have visitors and I fixed way too much food. Come and eat."

The director looked at me and I nodded. So, instead of touring the house, we turned around and went right back out. Old quilts were thrown on the ground. Everyone wanted to sit by me.

The kids fired questions like "Where are you from?" and "Are you going to come and live with us?" One of the younger-looking ones asked "Do you know that red and yellow make blue?"

I laughed and answered, "Gratis, I don't know and yes."

After lunch, most of the kids drifted off - some to study and some to play. One or two stayed, content to just hang around me - the "maybe, maybe not" new kid.

Eventually, the nun took the judge and me all through the house, from the first floor all the way up to the third. There were beds everywhere. Music drifted from behind doors that were closed and through ones that weren't. In a large den, several kids were watching cartoons. Down the hall, a couple of guys my age were putting a model airplane together. It looked like a lot of fun.

Eventually, we ended up in the kitchen where two nuns were mixing batter for what looked like a chocolate cake.

"We have two birthdays tomorrow: Katie L. and Katie P.. Now, isn't that funny? Two Katies born on the exact same day."

I nodded "yes" and tried to remember what I did on my last birthday. Nothing much, I guess.

Once we said our goodbyes, the judge asked me what I thought about the place.

"Not bad, not bad at all. Not like I thought it was going to be," I answered truthfully.

"I was hoping you might see it that way. Isn't it strange how things don't always match the way we envision them?" he asked.

"Yes. I just knew for sure that a boggy man would be hiding behind every door," I answered with a laugh.

"Why don't you think about it overnight," he suggested.

I didn't need to think about it. I already knew what my answer would be.

TWENTY-FOUR

SINCE THAT TIME

A lot has happened since that time. But then again, it's been thirty years or more. Yet, hardly a day goes by that I don't think about my decision and how it impacted my life. Most of all, I think about how good people made me who I am.

Mrs. Jordan died years ago. Her health had been declining for years, so it came as no surprise. On the day of her funeral, her son came back to town on account of Preacher Wilcox. He was the one who tracked him down.

After the funeral, I was surprised and touched to learn that everything the Jordan's owned was left to me in their will. No matter, it couldn't ever fill the empty hole in my heart, knowing both the Jordans were gone for good.

Even though their house and everything in it was now mine, I gave it to their son. Seemed only right. Who hasn't been in an argument or gotten crossed up with someone, only to regret it later? Just hard to go back and admit that you were wrong.

Mrs. Caldwell retired from teaching. Boyd, her husband and their three daughters moved back to

Atlanta to be near relatives. Every so often, I travel that way and think of their daughters like nieces. Sometimes, we all go to the theater or to a museum. Occasionally, they come to visit me in return.

Mrs. Reader is still at the library. She doesn't do a lot of the tugging and lifting of books like she use to do.

A couple of years ago, she threatened to quit altogether when they put in a computerized check-out system. The other librarians told me she actually did walk out that day but kept coming back to check on something or another and without really meaning to, she was back at work - same as usual. The whole thing was like it never happened in the first place.

Several years ago, the library basement was remodeled. I helped out quite a bit because Mrs. Reader wanted to preserve the history of Gratis for future generations. Since I was the one who sorted them in the first place, she needed me to help her get thing re-organized.

Throughout it all, Mrs. Reader was never able to locate the newspaper clipping of Mama again. Since the whole brooch-thing is long over with, I'm going to leave it at that.

In the middle of sifting through old records, I made a startling discovery. There was never any authorization to pay me for Story Hour but it wasn't hard to figure out Mrs. Caldwell put in a dollar and Mrs. Reader did the same. I wanted to say "thank you" but every time I tried, Mrs. Reader cut me off with "Nonsense. I'm sure these old records are wrong. You know how scattered I am and how things get misplaced." I guess that was her way of saying, "You're welcome."

When the Reinquists got too old to farm for a living, Jerry and his wife Sally put some money down and took over the place. In addition to apples, they planted pecans. Both crops have continued to be quite successful. We get together every now and then to laugh about the old days.

After graduating from high school, Carl joined the Navy and didn't come back until his step-daddy passed away. Once back, he took care of his aging mother but less than two years later, she was gone. Some say she died of a broken heart. Carl says "No such thing, more than likely – he beckoned and she obeyed.

On the day of her funeral, the funniest thing happened. A beautiful woman entered the church and walked right down front to sit with the family. She sat sobbing with her head in her hankie. None of us could imagine who this stranger was or why she was grieving to that extent.

As it turns out that she was from the north Georgia mountains and thought she was at the funeral of a childhood friend. She had taken the wrong turn and instead of being at a funeral in Monroe, she ended up in Gratis.

Carl is firmly convinced she was sent from God above, and that may be. Anyway, they've been married for over twenty years now and are still madly, deeply in love. Not only that, their three sons and one daughter never fail to point out, "Daddy is still walking on air."

I never dreamed that I would make it to college, but I did. I was awarded a track scholarship after graduating at the top of my class.

I ended up at the University of Georgia and loved

every minute of it. No one knew me as the poorest kid around. It was my first chance to be like everybody else. I was happy to be just "Bayou Brown – student".

But I wasn't like everyone else. I wasn't raised in a home with a mother and father. I didn't have brothers to fight with, or sisters to adore. I was raised by the goodness of people, not rich people, mind you - ordinary people doing extraordinary things for a dirty, skinny throwaway kid.

After graduation even though I tried to move in a different direction, I was pulled back.

How could I ever leave the best, the very best that life has to offer? How could I not grow old surrounded by people with a generous spirit that knew no bounds?

As for me and the decision I gave the judge outside *The Home* that day, I reckon was an immediate "no" and a gradual "yes".

Life is funny. Although, I spent years avoiding it, I was irresistibly pulled back to that large white house with the enormous shade trees. I didn't plan it that way but no matter how I tried to look the other way, there was no denying that it tugged at me.

So, when *The Home* ran an ad looking for a new administrator, I interviewed and got the job. That's where I've been to this very day. I guess sometimes the thing you think you don't want is the very thing you really do.

Working at *The Home* brought me in contact with Ailene Cunningham and her daughter Irene on a daily basis. Ailene and I patched up our differences and on more than one occasion, she's gone with me to put flowers on Mama's grave.

Irene and I married. I can't say that fireworks went off the first time we met again after college. It was a gradual thing. First, we were co-workers at *The Home*, then friends. Next, we were sweethearts. Eventually, man and wife. Though we've never had any kids of our own, we both feel that we have been richly blessed with the thirty or so who live with us every year at *The Home*.

Sometimes, we ride over to Monroe with Jerry and Sally or Carl and his wife. After all, where else can you get the best hot dogs east of the Mississippi?

I pretended for years, the man at the counter who whispered to Irene the day we became *Risk Takers* was my dad, he probably wasn't. Although, he did say, "The quiet one, meaning me, reminds me of myself years ago. Why don't you girls take a risk and see where it goes?"

In a way, I guess Irene continued to be a *Risk Taker*. After all, she picked me.

Mama's brooch that was the start of everything now belongs to Ailene. That may sound strange but it just feels like the right thing. Ailene tearfully apologized for taking it in the first place and I accepted her apology.

The brooch is a closed chapter in my life. That's not to say that it was necessarily all that bad. A lot of good came from it. There are some that say that before the day of confessions, Gratis was nothing more than a collection of people from all walks of life but afterwards, there was an unspoken bond which many feel continues to this very day.

The best part about it was that no one held it against Ailene. To them, it was simple. She took the brooch even though she shouldn't have. She knew it. Everyone else knew it, too.

I guess the real question is how long do you make someone suffer for a bad decision or a mistake. Do you hold it against them forever or do you eventually move on?

It took awhile but in Gratis the whole thing died down and pretty much went back to the way it had always been.

Every so often, Carl and I reminisce about the past. Irene keeps telling me that I need to write everything all down but I'm not sure anyone would believe it. Anyway, how could I possibly explain why I came back to *The Home* after years of struggling to stay clear of it?

The real reason is simple but true. I just wanted to make sure everyone still gets three squares a day.

They do.

55260492R00079

Made in the USA
Charleston, SC
25 April 2016